for Kella,
Happy Reading :)

THREE NIGHTS WITH A
ROCK STAR

AMBER LIN
SHARI SLADE

PRAISE FOR AMBER LIN'S BOOKS

"Amber Lin shows us that romance isn't just for the rich and shiny. Love can find its way even into the dark corners of the most damaged hearts."

—Tiffany Reisz, bestselling author

"Amber's work cuts deeper than that of anybody else I can think of—her prose is beautiful, the dark emotions are darker, the sex is sexier."

—Ruthie Knox, New York Times Bestselling Author

"She has a beautiful, atmospheric writing style and you're not going to find sentimental love here, nor are you going to find hearts and flowers. This is taut, compelling, thoughtful and also gritty, earthy and unembellished."

—Sinfully Sexy Book Reviews

"Oh and as for Amber Lin, well she was already on my shelf as a favourite Author of mine and yet again she proved just why. Her writing style is beautiful, flawless and so evocative you live and breathe her stories."

—TotallyBooked Blog

"Amber Lin has created an incredible story that is a captivating mix of redemption, love, and psychological suspense that I thoroughly enjoyed, and I highly recommend it to more adventurous readers!"

—The Autumn Review

"Since the release of Giving It Up, the first book in her Lost Girls series, I have been a die-hard fan of this author and have been singing her praises to everyone who wants to listen. Four full-length novels later and it is evident that Amber Lin's talent is not restricted to dark romances, she also writes wonderful steamy and sweet contemporaries."

—Swept Away by Romance

PRAISE FOR SHARI SLADE'S BOOKS

"In THE OPPOSITE OF NOTHING, Shari Slade takes the 'Just Friends' trope and injects it with such wry, authentic, achey longing that I became physically uncomfortable. GOD HOW I SQUIRMED. SO. MUCH. SQUIRMING."

—Lia Riley, author of Upside Down

"I love a friends to lovers story and I loved how the college life in this was real. Yes, there's new adult angst but there is also messy dorm rooms, stale Oreos and unrequited love."

—Wicked Little Pixie

"This is a great example of new adult fiction done right. Can't wait for the next one."

—Lexxi Callahan, author of Sweetened With a Kiss

"Slade's writing style and characterization is a cut above many of the novels I've recently read in the new adult and adult romance genre. Highly recommended, and I look forward to her next new adult read."

—Catherine Stine, author of Fireseed One

"I really enjoyed the dialogue in this story as I felt a connection to both characters. Their story is fresh, a bit young, and fun."

—She Reads New Adult

"Gorgeous prose and real characters. They weren't perfect looking or damaged beyond repair. They had flaws but both made every effort to overcome them and be independent."

—Megan Erickson, author of Make it Count

I swallowed planets
that fell from the sky.
I captured angels
and led them to die.

Let me lead you
down
into the belly of the beast.

Beast, Half-Life

CHAPTER ONE

Friday night

TWENTY DOLLARS FOR parking? Per night. And the garage was the budget-friendly option. Valet didn't even have the price listed. Resigned, Hailey dug in her purse for a twenty and handed it over. The booth attendant raised his eyebrow, giving her car a once-over. Well, okay. Message received. She clearly didn't belong at the ritzy hotel, even as a visitor.

It was true. She normally spent less than twenty dollars a day on food. And her old Toyota had broken down twice on the drive into Chicago. Heck, the booth attendant probably made more than she did. But if she was going to be stuck here for a few days, she'd have to adjust her standards a little bit. It was for a good cause.

A necessary cause.

The garage was filled to the brim, a gleaming array of BMWs, Porsches, and other brands she couldn't name. They looked like jewels on a velvet display case, her rusty hunk of steel an unseemly contrast.

She traveled lower, into the bowels of the hotel, and found an open space hiding in a corner. Her coupe managed to squeeze between the painted concrete wall and the metal Dumpster. She wrinkled her nose at the smell already seeping inside the car.

Holding her breath, she peeked at herself in the rearview mirror.

A stranger stared back at her. A stranger with heavy eyeliner and blue shadow. And glitter all over her face. The eye makeup had been on purpose. The glitter had been an unfortunate accident with the shimmer powder and a stuck lid.

She hadn't bothered to wash it off, though. It made her look fun and zany, like the kind of person who would take a dare and up the stakes. The kind of person who would crash a major label band's after-party. It made her look like a different person, and for the next few days that was who she would be.

Focus. She could do this. She *had* to do this.

The car door clattered against the metal wall of the Dumpster, leaving only a sliver of space. She sucked in her stomach and squeezed through—and heard an unfortunate rip. *Damn.* She glanced down. She'd torn her stockings. Her sister's stockings, technically.

Hailey was used to getting runs in her stockings at work. Chubby little hands with razor-sharp nails made it common. But this was more than a small run. This was a gaping hole right at her left ankle. Hazards of wearing fishnets, she supposed.

It seemed colder here even though the temperature shouldn't be much different than Lake Elkhart. Maybe it was the lack of blood circulation after driving for hours. Or maybe it was nerves. Either way, she felt chilled to the bone. She reached inside for the cardigan she always left stashed in her backseat. It never hurt to be prepared.

She followed the signs to the elevator bay, breathing a sigh of relief as she cleared the Dumpster's smelly radius. The button lit red while she waited.

Ding.

She wobbled as she moved in front of the elevator about to open. How did her sister wear these shoes, anyway? Reflective gold doors slid apart, revealing a couple. Having sex. Or almost having sex? She wasn't sure. But the rhythmic motions and clothes shoved aside certainly indicated…good Lord.

Their harsh breathing echoed in the elevator. They were moving, rubbing, grinding. A flash of pink skin. Hailey definitely shouldn't have seen anything pink, but she couldn't stop looking. Couldn't stop staring. Her eyelids were frozen, her whole body clamped into place, pinned under the weight of her own naïveté.

The guy looked up from the elevator floor. His heated gaze ran down her body and up again, and unlike the booth attendant, this guy seemed pleased with what he saw.

Her mouth hung open. She snapped it shut.

"Pardon me," she said inanely. As if *she* had been the one to interrupt them. Which, in a way, she had been.

His grin was feral. "Come on in. Water's fine."

Oh my God. "No, thank you. I'll catch the next one."

Of its own volition, her gaze wandered down the slope of his back to the guy's exposed ass, clenching and thrusting. She wasn't about to join in, but in some distant, terrifying way, the scene tugged at her.

The girl beneath him giggled as she watched Hailey from beneath heavy lids. "He calls it a joyride."

"I can see why," Hailey said faintly.

The elevator doors closed on their laughter. She stared at her own reflection once again. The elevator bay echoed silent, absent of gasped breaths and fabric rubbing against fabric.

So, that was different.

She took a deep breath of cool, stale air.

On the upside, she now felt totally awake after her long, drowsy drive. Way more effective than a jolt of caffeine could have been. Half-naked people rutting on the elevator floor were her own personal splash of water in the face.

On the downside, she wasn't sure she could pull off her plan anymore. She wasn't cut out for this. This was Chloe's scene. Chloe wouldn't have been freaked out by a couple having a good time. Though Hailey had no desire to imagine her sister going on a *joyride.*

Remembering her reaction, her stomach sank. *No, thank you.* Ugh. Could she be any more prim? She'd just been…shocked. Had she *ever* seen two other people having sex before? No. In real life, no. There had been a few wayward Internet searches she wasn't entirely sure were proper.

She stood in the musty alcove, torn by indecision. Should she still go up? What choice did she have?

Her phone beeped. She glanced at the screen to see a text from Chloe.

Pineapple and canadian bacon?

Her heart panged. It was a peace offering, that text. Things had been strained between them the past few days, after her sister's revelation. They had always been best friends or mortal enemies, constantly teasing or at each other's throats, so the quiet politeness had been unnerving.

The text also meant her sister hadn't found the quickly scrawled note letting her know that Hailey would be gone for a few days. The pizza delivery and C-rated movie would have to wait until she got back.

One good thing: the exchange steeled her resolve. Her spine straightened. She pressed the elevator button again and texted back for Chloe to eat without her.

She was doing this for her sister. Her only family. She needed to do it, or everything she'd worked toward in taking care of Chloe, in building a better life for them, would be for nothing. She had to, or history would repeat itself.

So when the reflective doors opened again, she stepped into the elevator. Stepped through the looking glass, where everything was upside-down and inside out, and so was she.

What she found was…disaster.

Hailey had imagined her arrival in the hotel several times during the long drive over. In her mind it would be more like storming a castle than pushing through heavy glass doors. In every fantasy she had been tough. Even fierce.

In none of them had she stumbled over a stranger who was halfway to puking into a lobby fern. And then he *was* puking. There were a few other people sprawled on couches or just right on the floor, but no one looked conscious. And certainly no one looked concerned by the sick man at her feet.

She knelt and awkwardly patted his back. He listed to the side and landed with his head in her lap.

Ugh. She fished in her purse for a wet wipe and pressed it into his hand. Those wipes always came in handy for runny noses or sticky hands. With a sleepy burp the man in her arms closed his eyes and appeared to fall asleep.

Should she…just leave him here?

That seemed wrong. But then again, he was hardly alone. There were a multitude of sleeping—or stoned?—bodies strewn around the sleek, modern lobby. It seemed a little early to have partied and collapsed by seven p.m., like they were her preschoolers who were wild all day and then crashed at a reasonable bedtime.

Despite the hefty price tag that surely accompanied such a

place, no attendant stood behind the glass-paneled counter. A swanky hotel like this one would have someone stationed all night long. Maybe they had fled the scene.

Maybe Hailey would be smart to follow suit.

But she couldn't leave. She hadn't spent the last ten years taking care of her sister only to mess it up now. Arguably she already *had* messed it up, but she was going to fix it. She wouldn't leave until it was fixed. She just had to find the lead singer—he went by the name of Lock—and appeal to his better nature…but first she had to figure out what to do with the passed-out guy in her lap.

From the wispy shadows down a corridor came the squeak of steps. At least someone here was awake and upright. And tall, she realized, listening to the slow, casual pace. Hopefully he would know where she could find Lock.

CHAPTER TWO

LOCK STORMED INTO the lobby. Moe had ganked his lucky guitar pick—again—and he was going to get it back. Even if it meant wading through the pile of half-naked bodies spread before him. The air was thick with sweat, bong water, bourbon, and vomit. His stomach should turn, but all he wanted to do was roll around in it. Like a stray dog.

No. He might be dirty, but he'd been sober for 372 days. Screwing that up was not an option.

His career—his life—depended on it. He knew too well how one misstep could destroy everything. He had the sex tape, the canceled tour dates and now the record label's sword of Damocles hanging over his head to prove it.

He tripped over Krist, who was sprawled on the floor in front of an empty upholstered chair, like he'd shot for the seat and given up a few steps short. His face pressed into the hotel lobby carpet, muffling his words. "The fuck, man?"

"Looking for Moe. You know where he landed?"

"Up some redhead's skirt." Krist rolled onto his back, exposing his inked stomach—the cover art from their first album—and the top of his junk. His pants were still open.

Lock nudged him in the ribs with his boot. "Zip it, man. And roll over. We don't need you pulling a Hendrix."

"Whatever, *bro*. You flashed your shit all over the Internet."

He winced. *Bro* was a reference to the weeklong hookup between Lock's mother and Krist's father in the endless '80s rock-star sex parade. They weren't really siblings—in fact, far from it. But they used the name as a reminder of their shared past. They'd both been castoffs on tour. Too young to party but old enough to want to. They'd picked up guitars and taught themselves—taught each other—to play. Screwing around with instruments they had no business touching. *Some things never change.* Krist hadn't called him *bro* in a long time. Not since before Lock had started fucking everything up, long before he'd *flashed his shit.* He hadn't chosen to do that. Someone had done it for him. But he'd owned it like it was all part of his master plan. What else was he supposed to do? *Bro.* It was a stalemate. The cold war within the Half-Life band.

He nudged Krist again. "I mean it, *bro.*"

Krist flipped him off but rolled over anyway. Lock wasn't in charge, but people usually did what he said. Usually. Since he'd—what did his agent call it?—*embraced sobriety.* Not fucking Moe. Where was that sneaky bastard? Lock wanted to embrace his balls with a vise.

The formerly gorgeous lobby was a pit. The label was going to bill them a fortune for this shit. And piss their pants with excitement. *Half-Life Bad Boys Trash Hotel, Orgy in Chicago Hilton.* Those headlines sold concert tickets. Sex, drugs and rock and roll, baby.

As long as *he* wasn't doing it. As long as it didn't go too far. They wanted the *illusion* of debauchery. The other guys could hold it together. For now. All Lock did was fall apart.

He followed the sound of dry heaves, and there was Moe. Cradled in the arms of some blonde who was rubbing his back. Was she humming a fucking lullaby?

"You're not a redhead." She wasn't. She wasn't a groupie

either. Groupies did not wear cardigans to hotel parties. Smoky shadow rimmed her eyes, but she still somehow looked like a Sunday school teacher sitting right in the middle of hell.

"Not the last time I checked." She shrugged and kept rubbing Moe's back. Definitely not a groupie. A groupie would've recognized him and dumped Moe like last week's trash. Unless she had a thing for drummers. It happened. That's all they were—fetishes that could be tried and discarded before the girls returned to the nice guys back home.

He gave her a lazy perusal. "What are you doing here?"

"I was—I was hoping to meet L-Lock. Do you know where I could find him?" Her pink lips quirked into a wide smile. False bravado. He knew that when he saw it too.

This might be entertaining. He pushed up the sleeve of his shirt, exposing his most photographed tattoo, a serpent coiled around an anatomical heart. She couldn't miss it. "You a big fan?"

"Oh, yeah. Really big fan."

She was lying. And sober. Who sat in the middle of this mess sober? She could be some weird star fucker, looking to hook up with anyone famous just to say she did. *That can be arranged.* Though she wouldn't be telling anyone, not after she signed his agreement. Not without paying a hefty penalty and having her name raked through the tabloids.

He forced a wide yawn, flashing his trademark tongue stud. No recognition. Maybe she didn't worship at his alter; she just worshipped celebrity. Worship. She looked like her kind of worship involved hymnals and psalms.

A flash of her on her knees—*not in prayer*—made him waver. This might be more than entertaining; it might be fun. It had been a long time since he'd had fun.

"I can take you to him. If you're not too busy." He waved

his hand at Moe, his lucky guitar pick all but forgotten.

"Help me with him?" She tried to force Moe from her lap, but he was 200 pounds of uncooperative asshole. Lock grabbed his drummer by the shoulders and lifted his upper body away from…the church mouse. She was probably a Penelope or a Polly. Pure.

"What's your name?"

"Hailey. Thanks. I wasn't expecting to find everyone crashed already. Do you always party until you puke by seven p.m.?" She pulled something out of her purse. A wet nap? And turned around to bend over Moe.

Without a lump of drummer covering half her body, he was shocked to find black fishnets covering her legs. And a short denim skirt barely covering her ass. None of it suited her.

A costume.

"Didn't you hear, fan girl? The new single went platinum today. They started celebrating at noon. Anyone can party at midnight, it takes a real rock star to get it done in the daylight. Besides, this is half-time. They'll rally for another round."

"Oh," she said faintly. Then she wiped Moe's mouth and rolled him onto his side. Who was this chick?

He held out his hand, intrigued. Would she break character first or would he? "Follow me, Hailey. Let me lead you down into the belly of the beast."

And then he knew, without a doubt, she wasn't a groupie. That lyric. A real groupie would've come on the spot, right in her fucking panties. He couldn't count how many times random fan girls begged him, *Say it say it say it.* He never did. Why the hell had he said it now?

CHAPTER THREE

HAILEY FOLLOWED HIM down the hallway he'd come from. *Into the belly of the beast,* she thought with amusement. It had been hard to suppress her smile when he'd first said the words. She'd heard the phrase used ironically, of course, but he'd been heartbreakingly serious. And he had watched so carefully for her reaction. Luckily she had years of experience with preschoolers telling her all sorts of wild things. She knew how to keep a straight face.

"What did you say your name was?" she asked.

He stopped abruptly and turned, eyes narrowed.

She stumbled and barely avoided running into him. Her breath caught. It struck her suddenly how close their faces were. He was tall, and so was she on these ridiculous platform heels she'd borrowed from her sister. This close, she could see silver in the dusting of dark scruff along his jaw, even though he looked closer to her age. It seemed to suit him. He was metallic all over, from the tiny flecks of gold in his eyes to the sleek onyx ink tattooed on his arm.

And the peek of a silver piercing in his tongue when he spoke.

She'd never known a tongue piercing could be sexy. She wasn't sure why it was sexy now either, except that it just hinted at so much…sensual knowledge. And she'd always had a yearning for knowledge.

"I didn't," he said curtly, responding to her question. But when he continued forward, he spoke without looking at her. "You can call me Keaton."

"Oh," she said, somewhat breathless as she hurried to catch up.

The heels made her wobble like a newborn fawn, gangly and uncertain on her legs. He noticed, she knew, glancing back ever so slightly as he walked, lashes veiling his eyes. Though he was kind enough not to comment. And kind enough to take her to Lock without asking too many questions. A kind man, then.

She felt a sort of kinship with him, with *Keaton*. He was the only one here, besides her, who was fully clothed and sober. She, too, was used to being the responsible one. The one slightly apart from the rest.

Maybe it was presumptuous to think she could relate to a man who wore the rock-and-roll trappings like a second skin. But she knew as well as anyone that clothes were just camouflage. She'd had to sneak this entire outfit from her sister's closet, since her preference for pastels would hardly fit in here.

He stopped in front of an elevator and swiped his hotel key card. The doors opened immediately. At least no writhing bodies met her sight. Even the memory of them made her cheeks heat.

Keaton held the door and gestured her inside the empty elevator, the movement faintly mocking. Inside, the carpet tilted her heels every which way, and she clung to the gilded railing as he pressed the button for the top floor.

The penthouse. Of course Lock would be staying in the best room. And of course Chloe would be awed by such glamour.

No, she was being unfair. Chloe had obsessed over Lock

and the entire band for years. So when she'd secured the summer gig selling merchandise—or as Chloe called it, merch—on their tour, Hailey had tried to be happy for her sister, she really had. Even though it meant forgoing the extra summer classes they'd planned so Chloe could finish college sooner. Even though she called for Hailey to wire her money after a particular incident with a vending machine thrown out a window.

Even when Chloe came home pregnant.

God, even then Hailey had pasted on a smile. This was a *blessing*. She was almost sure about that. She would *make* it a blessing. But then, the final straw. The father wasn't going to be involved. He wasn't even going to help, not financially, not emotionally. He wanted no part of the child's life. And Chloe wouldn't tell her who the father was. She wanted to let the whole thing drop, when she and Hailey had been raised without a father and hardly a mother either, and they knew how painful it was. How desolate.

Hailey wasn't going to let that happen.

The elevator gave a muted *ding*, and the doors slid open. Directly into someone's living room. The kind of opulent, expansive place Hailey had only ever pictured on the glossy pages of a magazine. She hadn't even *bought* the magazine. She'd flipped through it in line at the grocery store and then guiltily returned it before checkout because who had $3.99 to spend on envy? But this was the real thing.

Like the half-naked bodies in the elevator—no longer pictures but the real thing.

She forced herself inside, hovering near the elevator even as it shut behind her.

Keaton showed no such hesitation. He strolled in like he'd been here a thousand times before. She supposed, since Lock trusted him with a key card, he probably had. Maybe he was an assistant of some kind. He went to a large bar and popped the lid of a Coke. No vending machines for penthouse residents.

He cocked the bottle toward her. "You want one?"

She shook her head, taking a hesitant step forward. "Do you know when Lock will be here?"

He sprawled into a large leather chair, one leg over the square arm, and took a sip of his drink. Chicago's twinkling nightscape framed him from behind. He looked so incongruously regal, sitting there, like a king surveying all he owned. And she knew, with a sinking feeling, what he was going to say before he did.

"Sweetheart, you're looking at him."

HER SHOULDERS SLUMPED, and her mouth settled into a disconcerting line of determination. The look on her face. She looked…resigned. He'd wanted to shock her, to watch her fluster and backpedal.

"Not what you expected?" he asked.

"No, you're exactly what I expected. I don't know why I didn't realize sooner. It's not like I've never seen your picture. I'm a little embarrassed. Do you mind if I sit?"

He nodded, still intrigued. She didn't lie or try to make herself look better. She just told the truth. What else might she say?

Her gaze darted around the room, a mouse scanning for danger, and she settled on the edge of a chaise lounge across from him. Then she took off her shoes—actually took off her shoes—and rubbed her stockinged feet. Worked her thumb deep into the arch, sighing. He felt it in his groin.

"Gosh, my feet hurt. I don't know how my sister wears these things. If I put anything other than a sneaker or a croc near my toes, they just curl up in terror. Like the Wicked Witch of the East. Taking off my shoes is my favorite part of the day. That and my bra. Oh."

"By all means, take that off too."

She bit her lip and flushed. He knew she regretted that last admission as soon as it was out of her pretty mouth. She didn't look like the kind of girl who discussed her underwear in mixed company, but he couldn't resist pushing. This nervous babble was getting more interesting by the minute. The tantalizing peek of her bare toes through the fishnet was getting more interesting too.

He watched her school her features, bring herself back to calm and dignity. It was so much like what he did before he went onstage. Only in reverse. She steadied; he frenzied.

She took a deep breath. "I'd appreciate it if you didn't tease me. It isn't nice."

Her quiet reprimand brought him up short. No one had expected niceness from him, ever. He'd grown up on tour with his parents, rock royalty who'd lived fast and died not quite as young as they'd expected. He'd been treated alternately like a tiny king and luggage. He'd had almost everything he wanted and nothing he needed. He wouldn't know where to begin…being nice. "I'm not teasing. I'm being a good host. Seeing to your comfort. I'll even take it off for you."

She shook her head like he'd offered her another unwanted soda. So she wasn't here to try and fuck him. Why did that make his dick hard?

"I have a problem—a private, family matter—and I'd like your help."

He leaned back in the chair, inhaling the leathery scent, and rubbed his eyes. Of course she wanted something. A signed photograph? A vial of some bodily fluid? A sweaty T-shirt worn onstage? Exhaustion settled over him like a lead blanket. "What do you want?"

"Last month you bought my sister a bus ticket home. She toured with you this summer. She's…"

"She's what? Sorry she left? If she got a ticket home, it's because she needed to leave. I doubt she'd be welcome back, even if you do plead her case. And I don't buy tickets. Our tour manager might."

"She's pregnant."

So it was *that* scam again. This was part of the reason he had his agreement. No questionable paternity suits for him. Not anymore. He knew exactly who he fucked, when, and for how long. He had them stored in a file, and since he hadn't added to that in file nine months, he knew it wasn't this girl's transient sister. "Not by me. Not my problem."

"I didn't say it was yours. I'm pretty sure it isn't, because she won't talk about the father. She'd be shouting it from the rooftops if it was you. You're a god in her eyes."

"I'm no god. A demon, maybe." Keeping starry-eyed groupies from broadcasting his conquests was another reason for his agreement. Too often their excitement turned sour, the fantasy never quite matching the reality. Turned out he didn't magically become one of their nice guys when they fucked him, like some frog getting kissed. He'd written "Scorned" after a particularly grueling bout of tabloid vengeance.

Her soft brown eyes raked over his body. He could almost feel her gaze searching for scales and a tail. So fucking earnest. He wished he could sprout horns on the spot, to make her sad smile falter. "I was hoping you'd be able to help me find the father."

Now he was shocked. "You want me to interview my band? My crew? Pass her picture around at sound check? That isn't how it works."

"Nothing like that. We don't want it public. We both work for our church, and a scandal would be awful."

"Church?" He nearly snorted his soda, the bubbles tickling the back of his throat. "I'm surprised you didn't burst into flames downstairs. What do you do at church? No, let me guess. Sunday school?"

She pursed her lips. "Well yes. But that's volunteer work. Chloe volunteers with the youth group. My paid job is in the attached child-care center."

Of course. Another person paid to care. Worried about her job. "I can see why you'd want to keep this quiet."

"I think if I can talk to some of the people here, I might be able to figure it out. Quietly. I could blend in? Like a groupie? Just for a few days. So I can convince him to do the right thing."

A few days to ask around and figure out who her sister had fucked. Without it becoming public knowledge. Un-freaking-likely. Her plan was as thin as the air in the nosebleeds at Madison Square Garden, and judging from the desperation in her eyes, she knew it. But family could drive people to crazy depths; he knew all about that. For that and many reasons, he should throw her out, maybe even call the cops. This had stalker written all over it, but he couldn't hold back the grin spreading across his face as it clicked in his mind, exactly what he was going to do. He had so few vices left. "Stand up. Let me look at you."

She rose slowly. "Maybe I will take that drink. What do people drink when they have no idea what they're doing? Beer? Tequila?"

"Beer is for barbecues. Tequila is for bad decisions. And whiskey is for all-purpose adjustment. It's what I always reached for when I drank. But I can't help you drown your troubles in booze. Or are you looking for liquid courage?"

"No, I just—" The jut of her chin told him courage was exactly what she'd been looking for. He cast a glance at the bar, cleared of all alcoholic beverages prior to his arrival per his agent's instructions. Not even a bottle of bitters. Like he'd ever been that desperate.

"You won't find a drop of that here. I can call downstairs—"

"No, it's fine. It's not like I'm really a drinker." She shivered. "I hate the taste."

He regretted ever acquiring it.

She'd never pass as a groupie. Not even with her ripped fishnets and glitter fetish. She'd looked too horrified, too out of place in the middle of all the debauchery downstairs. And tonight was tame. But if she was with him? How badly did she want this particular all-access pass?

"You can stay, but I'll need you to agree to a few terms first."

"Whatever you want."

"Yes, that's number one on the list."

HAILEY FORCED HERSELF to stand still for his leisurely perusal. Even when he stood and stalked toward her, she managed to hold on to her dignity—whatever dregs she had left after donning these clothes and almost falling on her face. But his smile hit her like a blast of heat, blinding her, scalding her. He looked far too pleased with himself, like a man about to get everything he wanted. And her shaky insides warned she might just give it to him.

"What do you mean?" she asked, proud her voice didn't quaver too much.

"You want to stay here while we're in Chicago," he said. "To stay here for three days, to blend in so that no one questions why you're here. To ask questions, poke around."

Yes, that was exactly what she wanted. So why did her nod feel like surrender? As if she'd agreed to his terms before she even knew them. But then maybe she *did* know what his terms would be. His eyes spoke the words his lips had yet to say. There were volumes of gold-flecked pages filled with all that sensual knowledge. They promised delight and, even better, a hard bite to the exchange. Where the men she had been with were a fresh spring breeze, he stood before her like the calm before the storm, his eyes darkening clouds.

"Can you..." She licked her lips. His gaze tracked the movement, making her feel hunted. "Can you help me?"

His expression softened. Just the slightest degree, but it was enough to slow the hammering of her heart. This was the same kind man she'd met in the lobby. Desire had given him a rough edge, turning his loping gait into a prowl, making his nostrils flare—scenting her. But he was still kind inside.

When he didn't answer, she searched for whatever strength she might have found. *You want...* he'd said, listing *her* terms. Only *his* terms were left to be stated. A negotiation, then. But even as she thought the words, an image flashed through her mind, a gazelle caught from behind, the vicious beauty of her captor feasting in a *National Geographic* special.

"What do you want?" she whispered, and somehow the wall was at her back. He was at her front...crowding her...embracing her?

"You," he snarled. "Under me. Over me. On your knees in front of me. I get full artistic license to your body for three days."

His words pounded her like hail, leaving dents and then pooling in the hollows left behind. They drowned out the rest of the world and shook the floor. She began to shake too—but her gaze remained locked with his. The shaking was on the inside, fear and a strange longing warring inside her, a battle to the death. She stood frozen, caught in his sights and too terrified to run. Too curious to walk away.

He stepped back, sending a wash of crisp hotel air over her body. She sucked in a breath and immediately missed the earthy scent of him.

"And you," he continued conversationally, "will have total access to play Nancy Drew in the hotel. That is, whenever I'm not using you."

Her body lit up when he said the word *using*. It imploded on *you,* spoken with such self-assured possession. What was wrong with her that she wanted to be used? Maybe because she wanted to be free to enjoy sex, to really explore it, for the first time in her tame little life. Maybe because *he* would be the one using her, and he seemed like he would know just what to do with her.

This was a bad idea. For reasons that weren't quite coming to her at the moment. But she knew it was bad. If she'd said it once, she'd said it a thousand times to her preschoolers: don't make decisions when you're angry. Though she wasn't angry. She was concerned. And frustrated. And…

God, Chloe, why? After I worked so freaking hard so you could start college, why couldn't you be more careful?

Okay, she might be angry.

She swallowed. So maybe this weekend could be for her

too. She *would* find the baby's father, but she'd also find something for herself.

With a deep breath, she struggled for levity. A lopsided tilt of her lips was all she could manage. "Where do I sign?" she joked.

His grin widened, revealing an even row of white teeth. The Cheshire cat had just such a smile. "I'm so glad you asked. I have blank copies of my contract in the side table. Right next to the lube."

CHAPTER FOUR

C HLOE STARED AT the white oval, willing a second blue line not to appear. It did. Just like it had for the last seven strips. She'd also been disappointed by a red circle, a pink plus, and the word *Not* never forming in front of the word *Pregnant*.

She tossed the current plastic stick into the little trash can overflowing with cardboard packaging and instructions. Stupid. She was stupid for taking so many tests, as if they could all be wrong, as if the doctor's office could have been wrong.

It was just like when her mother left behind that hastily scrawled phone number. Chloe had called the number again and again. Even when Hailey shook her head and said Mom wasn't coming back, Chloe had waited until her sister went to sleep and then dialed the number so many times she could hear the disconnected chime in her dreams. Her sister had always been smarter.

Getting pregnant at nineteen was stupid too, but Chloe couldn't think about that right now. She was still here, in this place of uncertainty and possibilities. The *maybe I'm somehow not pregnant* possibility.

But she was. She'd known it since she missed her first period while on tour with Half-Life. She'd felt something, *someone* inside her, even though the Internet claimed it was too soon to know. In denial, she'd packed up and boarded a Greyhound without even sending so much as a text to…well, without telling a soul.

Sitting on the toilet, she put her head in her hands.

Options. She needed to consider her options. There should be a flowchart for this situation that asked you questions and led you to the right answer.

At the very top it would ask, *What would you say if a cute guy offers to teach you guitar?* Yes.

If he plays you a song about love lost and then kisses you, what then?

If you're both drunk on lust, and he just wants to see what it would be like, just wants to feel you without anything between you, would you do it?

But she couldn't blame it on him. She'd wanted to feel him too, and it had felt insanely good, impossibly sweet, like for the first time she wasn't having sex, she was making love. He'd pulled out, but not soon enough, obviously.

Stupid.

She sighed. The next rectangle in the flowchart would ask, *Did you get pregnant?* And yes, she had. She could admit that now, after using up an entire shelf at the drugstore.

Next box in the chart. *Do you want an abortion?* No, not when she already *felt* the little alien inside her. *Adoption?* Better, but she wasn't sure about that either. Her mother had left them, but Chloe had been okay because she had Hailey. Hailey to make sure she did her homework and Hailey to set her curfew. Hailey to hold her when she came home crying because she was pregnant. She couldn't be sure her child would have that. And she refused to make Hailey be a mother to another child she hadn't given birth to. So, the only person Chloe could count on to be a mother to this child was herself.

She *wanted* to be a good mother to her child. Strange but true.

All she had to do, then, was figure out how to be Hailey.

Where was her sister anyway? *Weren't you just saying you'd rely on yourself, not her?* Okay, but still, it was weird. The ever-responsible Hailey had disappeared without telling Chloe where she'd gone.

Chloe left the bathroom and stood in the open doorway to Hailey's empty room as if it might hold a clue, as if a brochure to Tahiti might have been left on the nightstand. Maybe with the tagline *Stressed because your baby sister got herself knocked up? Well, come on down to our resort and relax.* Chloe wouldn't even blame her.

But it was weird.

The bed was made. Of course. The nightstand was clear of everything except a book her sister had been reading, with its pages dog-eared. The closet looked undisturbed, with not enough missing to really suggest a long trip. Even those sensible green crocs were in their proper cubby. Hailey loved those crocs.

Chloe pulled her phone from her pocket and found her sister's name. *Seriously, where are you?*

A few minutes later the response came. *I told you, I'm fine. Don't worry.*

Well of course she was fine. This was Hailey, who always had her shit together, who always did the right thing. But it didn't really answer the question. Where the hell was she?

A little bubble on the screen indicated she had other text messages from someone else. She didn't want to look. She wasn't going to look.

She looked.

Hey, I heard you left the tour

Did something happen? Are you okay?

Call me

She winced. Fuck. She could just imagine his expression too, a mixture of frustration and concern. She hadn't even been sure he cared about her when she left. Maybe she'd just been a convenient lay.

She was used to being a convenient lay, really.

Between the guys at her high school and the random hookups at concerts, it had been a leapfrog game of sex that she'd found exciting at first. And then just tiring. Except for him. He'd been…something different. Something real, until she'd gotten scared and split.

She texted back: *I'm okay. Call you soon.* And then shut off her phone. Which was cowardly, but that was what he got for dealing with the irresponsible sister. Anyway, she would tell him. She'd have to.

Tonight maybe.

With a final, fruitless glance, she left her sister's bedroom and went into her own. She was ready to fall onto the bed and possibly hide under the covers for the next nine months when something from the closet caught her eye.

Unlike Hailey's tidy closet, Chloe's was overflowing with clothes and bling. Satiny halter tops and a tiara. Heavy metal T-shirts and Mardi Gras beads. She kept most of her clothes for clubbing near the back. She just bunched them into a ball and threw them into a Rainbow Brite bucket. Except now they were all rolled into little symmetrical piles, and there was only one person who could fold fishnet stockings that neatly.

What the hell had Hailey been doing in her closet? They'd agreed never to cross each other's thresholds, as if they were state lines and violation an act of war. Sure Chloe still secretly borrowed clothes occasionally, like that cardigan when she'd been Sandra Dee for Halloween. But Hailey never even wore clothes like Chloe's, especially not the party stuff. It didn't make sense.

She picked through all her clothes and found her platform boots missing. Her stilettos too. God, Hailey would break an ankle in those. Chloe almost had several times. Her slinky black dress was gone. A few tops. Possibly a pair of acid-washed jeans.

She sat amid the textile wreckage and shook her head. The world was turning upside down. Here she was at home alone on a Friday night. Hailey was out someplace mysterious, past curfew. Well, one thing was for sure, wherever her sister was, she was looking damn hot.

And Chloe knew where she needed to go.

HAILEY SAT AT the gleaming dining room table, alone in the expansive room. She bit her lip and stared at her sister's smiling pic on the phone screen. She had avoided calling Chloe on the way here, knowing it would change her mind. But the text messages and voice mails had already started coming. If Hailey didn't answer for the whole weekend—the full three days of the contract—Chloe would genuinely worry.

With a sigh, Hailey pressed the CALL button.

Her sister sounded cautious. "Did you get lost picking up a movie?"

"No, I...I forgot about movie night." She grimaced. As explanations went, that one was weak.

There was a weighted silence. "You mean the movie night we've had every Friday for three years. *That* movie night?"

"Except for when you were gone on tour," Hailey retorted,

but it was a cheap shot. Her sister was *pregnant,* for God's sake. Hailey should be there, making sure she was comfortable, making sure she ate enough.

And she would…right after this.

This was for the best. This was *necessary.* She had to believe that, because the alternative felt too much like history repeating itself. Absent parents and struggling to get by. No, Hailey wouldn't let that happen.

She'd just have to say it quickly, like tearing off a Band-Aid. "I'm in Chicago. At the hotel where the band is staying."

"*What?*"

"I know you said to drop it, that the father wasn't interested and you're fine with that, but *I'm* not fine with that. It's not right for the baby to grow up without a father."

"You realize this is the twenty-first century, right? There are women who have babies alone on purpose."

"Well, you aren't one of them. And those women probably have careers and…you know, money. They aren't nineteen years old and dropping out of college, with no plan for their life."

A huff of breath. "No, tell me how you really feel. I can take it."

Her stomach twisted with guilt. "I'm sorry. I didn't mean it like that." That sounded lame, so she added, "You know I love you."

God, how could that sound lamer?

"I love you too," Chloe said with that pouting voice, which helped strengthen Hailey's resolve. Chloe was practically a baby. And now she was having a baby. *Someone* had to do *something,* and this desperate race over Illinois's plains was the only plan she'd come up with at five p.m. today.

"Look, just tell me who the father is, and I'll talk some

sense into him."

"I can't believe you're even in Chicago. Who are you, and what you have done with my sister?"

"Even if he doesn't want to be involved with the child—after I've talked to him—he has a financial obligation. We should talk to a lawyer."

"That's definitely not happening."

"Chloe, this isn't money for you or me. This is money for the child."

"Can you please stop saying *the child* the same way you'd say *the plague* or *Voldemort*. He can hear you, you know."

"No, he can't—" Hailey let out an exasperated sound because Chloe was just messing with her. That was Chloe, always casual, always chill. But this whole situation? Not casual. And Hailey was feeling a long way from chill.

"Tell me his name," Hailey said sternly. It was her *mom voice*, as Chloe called it. Usually right before she said the words…

"You can't make me."

"I'm going to find him anyway. You're just making this harder."

"No, I'm making it *impossible*. As it should be. You're never going to find him."

It felt like a challenge. Was it supposed to feel like a challenge? Did Chloe secretly want her to find the father and convince him to help? Regardless, it was happening. Starting with this contract, which would give her the access she needed. Not to mention a place to stay in the swanky hotel that was probably booked solid.

"I'm going to find out who the father is," she said softly. Fiercely. "And he's going to help."

That definitely came out like a challenge. Hailey didn't *want* this to be a sibling-rivalry thing, but maybe it was too late for that. No matter how many times she'd said *do your homework* or *please don't graffiti our living room wall,* she was still a sister. Not a parent.

Chloe sighed. "Oh, Sis. I love that you want to help me. I just hate the way you're doing it."

Hailey swallowed hard as she stared down at the printed sheets of paper in front of her. This was her own personal gauntlet, walking on the fire of her secret desires. She'd have to give Lock whatever he wanted—and get what she wanted in return. She hated it too. But she also kind of loved it.

"I'll be home in a couple of days," Hailey said. "In the meantime, make sure you eat enough. And go to sleep early."

Chloe snorted. "In your dreams."

Somewhat reassured, Hailey ended the call. At least that much was the same between them. Because so much else had changed. On a typical Friday night Hailey would be throwing popcorn at Chloe while her sister chatted through the movie. She'd read two chapters of her library book and go to sleep by eleven. Whereas today…what *was* she doing? It was hard to tell, even with the words spelled out in black-and-white. The gleaming sheets of paper with crisp ink might as well have been a crumbling stone wall painted with hieroglyphs. Strings of symbols her mind couldn't comprehend.

Confidentiality Agreement, it said in bold letters at the top. And right here, she had to come to terms with the fact that he'd been serious about the contract. A real piece of paper, signed by both parties and filed…where? The Department of Rock-Star Relations? The Ministry of the Rich and Famous?

But farther down the words grew stranger. Her brain turned to mush, unable to process the bluntness of *bodily available* and *kink allowances.* She had, in the heat of the moment, agreed to do anything with him. Anything *for* him. But both her arousal and impulsiveness had deserted her now. She shuddered under the draft of air-conditioning above the desk.

Most of the contract was in legalese, things about nondisclosure and proprietary obligations.

She was supposed to read and sign this thing. A simple exchange, that's all it was.

She'd get to stay here and find Hailey's lover—and more importantly, convince him not to be a deadbeat father. And in return, she'd share Lock's bed. Something she wanted to do anyway.

At least she *had* wanted to. Now she was wondering whether she had what it took. Like maybe she should stretch and do push-ups before putting on her pjs. And oh God, her pjs! The threadbare old camisole and shorts she'd packed would look ridiculous in this place.

Taking a fortifying breath, she read the rest of the contract. *No monies will be exchanged.* So she wasn't going to get paid for having sex with him—should she be grateful she wasn't sacrificing her morals?

Or offended she didn't warrant a tip?

She might be going mad. This was all some weird, gritty Alice in Wonderland. She'd fallen down the hole, into a land where grinning cats led her up elevators and mad hatters invited her to share a Coke. *Off with her head,* the Queen of Hearts would say, and God. God. She was so screwed.

"You haven't signed it yet," he said from behind her, his breath caressing the back of her neck, sending shivers down her spine. "Having second thoughts?"

Oh, second and third and forty-seventh thoughts. "No, I just…I always read contracts before I sign them."

"Of course you do. I bet you balance your checkbook every Sunday too."

Hah, she did not. Unless he counted the spreadsheet she updated with the downloadable statements from her bank. Which he probably would. But there was nothing wrong with that. Money management was an important life skill.

She hated money management. She hated the downloadable statements and the spreadsheets. She did them so that Chloe could go to college—except her sister had never cared that much about her classes. She did the spreadsheets so that she wouldn't end up like her mother, accepting a "date" to make rent. And most of all, she did them because she didn't know how to stop. She'd never learned how to stop being responsible and boring. She'd never learned how to live.

With shaky hands, she picked up the pen and signed her name at the bottom.

"Don't look so terrified," he said, scrawling his name beside hers. "This is going to be fun."

Exactly what she was afraid of. She had lived her life buttoned-up and tucked away. She never saw anything to long for or experienced anything to regret. It was a kind of stasis that had helped her focus on raising her sister and keeping their tiny family unit going.

Finding out about her sister's pregnancy had torn Hailey right out of her neat little box. She'd been so focused on raising Chloe that she had barely realized she was a woman now. So when was Hailey going to stop playing surrogate? Soon there would be another child to help raise, another kid who wasn't exactly hers but was still her responsibility. When was Hailey going to start living?

And once she started, once she knew how sweet it could be, how would she stop?

CHAPTER FIVE

TIM REACHED FOR the light pull dangling from the storage-closet ceiling, but before he could tug it, someone stepped into the darkness behind him.

Not someone. *Chloe.*

The door clicked shut. The strong scent of tempera paint and oak tag mingled with her vanilla perfume. His fingers curled around the frayed ribbon. He should pull it—*let there be light*—but he couldn't. She'd be able to see him, see how much he wanted what he could not have. "You shouldn't be in here."

"I need to talk to you." Her fingertips landed softly on his shoulder, and he held his breath. One second. Two. A few moments more and the heat of her touch might leave scorch marks on the white cotton of his button-down. He'd stopped wearing T-shirts to church functions weeks ago. Even with his beard and his height, he had blended too well with the kids in the youth group.

"Let me find the board games, and then we can talk in the activity room." He pawed at the shelves, searching for the familiar box by touch, desperate for her to leave him in peace.

"Nobody gives a shit about Yahtzee, Pastor Tim." The light clicked on, and he fumbled. A box of Popsicle sticks clattered to the floor.

"Don't call me that. I'm not a pastor." He wasn't. Youth

ministry leader, sure. Pastor, no. She did that on purpose, to rile him. She'd done it for years, but it had only started to bother him this past year. She'd graduated from high school and taken over the junior youth group for the summer. They were sort of coworkers now, and what had once been a sweet schoolgirl crush had taken on a dangerous edge.

Possible but impossible. *Torture.*

When she'd left town with that band, he'd thought it was over. She'd go live the wild life he couldn't give her, and he could unbury himself from all the guilt. He dropped to his knees, scrambling to pick up the sticks, certain that any minute someone else would fling open the closet door and catch them—doing what, exactly? Organizing supplies? He wasn't doing anything wrong. Not this time.

She crouched beside him. "Let me help."

"You should get back out there, make sure the younger kids aren't staging a coup." The teens were trouble enough, but the tweens could make a young man go prematurely gray with the pranks they tried at a lock-in. Not that he'd found any silver himself. He checked, though, more often as he crept closer to thirty.

"They've already dropped spiders in the chip bowl—don't worry; they're plastic. And you might want to check your sleeping bag for ice cubes. You can always share mine. They know better than to prank me." She shoved a handful of sticks into the box he held, and brushed her thumb over the inside of his wrist, tracing the infinity symbol tattooed there. His hand shook. Like she'd never left.

"You're supposed to stop the pranks, not catalog them."

"They're harmless." She held his gaze, brow arched in question, thumb still pressed to his wrist. She had to feel his pulse now, the unmistakable *thump thump thump* hammering beneath his skin.

"I'm not sharing your sleeping bag." He'd take a bath in ice cubes first. The town would run him out on a flaming pitchfork if he even looked too long at Chloe's sleeping bag. *Off Limits*. It practically flashed neon above her head. She'd been one of his charges. No amount of grown-up, legal, or willing would change that.

"Of course not. Then everyone would know you like me." She licked her lips.

"I don't. Like you. I mean, of course I like you, you're lovely and smart, but we can't. Oh crap—"

The shock of her mouth, warm and wet against his, stunned him into silent acquiescence. Her fingers didn't scorch his shirt now; they raked over his shoulders as she pushed herself into his arms. A milk crate full of Sunday school workbooks shoved into the small of his back. A dull pain, overwhelmed as liquid heat coursed through his body, crowding out thought, mingling with the dread coiled in his belly.

The Popsicle sticks clattered to the floor again.

God help him, he kissed her back, unable to resist slipping his tongue into the apple-sweet depths of her mouth.

"Seven minutes in heaven," she gasped against his cheek as she grabbed his hand and guided it to her breast. "We can have that, can't we?"

The hard point of her nipple jutted against his palm through the fabric of her top. She felt so good. The soft weight of her pressed into his fingers. He groaned, erection already straining the fly of his jeans. He might not go to jail, but he was probably going to hell.

It took every ounce of his resolve to end the contact. He blew out a breath, slow and measured, and squeezed his eyes shut. A coward. "I'm so sorry, Chloe. This is wrong."

Cool air washed over him as she pulled away. Hurt filled her expression like he'd never seen before. Like he'd never imagined. So confident, so damn gorgeous he'd never thought she *could* be hurt. She was perfect, and she could do much better than her old youth leader. Her pain was like a lance, like a hundred of them, and they stabbed at him until his mouth opened. He wanted to tell her he was sorry, how much he loved her, how they just couldn't ever be together—

"I'm pregnant."

CHLOE SUCCESSFULLY AVOIDED Tim through two rounds of Yahtzee before he asked her to help him set up snacks. Just an excuse to get her alone, and nope, she had an urgent dodgeball game she needed to coordinate in the gym. Anything, anything but to face him after her blurted revelation in the closet.

She didn't know the best way to break this news to a guy, but that wasn't it. And immediately after her ill-timed confession, she'd left. Darted into the center of the group, using the kids as a shield so she wouldn't have to face Tim's judgment. She couldn't even look him in the eye. Even though he had done just as much as she had to create the baby. Even though he'd been a willing, eager participant at the time. But it was always the girl who got blamed, wasn't it? She'd been coming to Sunday school most of her life. She knew the stories.

Now her shields, her charges had abandoned her. Once the sweet smell of chocolate chip cookies permeated the gym, they'd dropped the colored kickballs in place and run to eat the cookies fresh from the oven.

She hadn't minded. Collecting the balls had given her an excuse to stay behind. It had given her an excuse to stay behind, to collect the balls. To hide in the storage room, breathing in rubber and disinfectant. To panic. She was panicking. God, why had she thought she could do this? Go about her role as one of the youth group helpers when she could barely help herself? Or have a calm, grown-up conversation with Tim about the situation when she didn't feel grown-up? And she certainly wasn't calm.

"Chloe?"

Shit. That was Tim, looking for her.

The worry in his voice was like a splash of ice water. It stole her breath and bent her over—and that was how he found her, head in her hands. The wooden bench squeaked as he sat beside her. His warmth suffused her hip and all along her body.

It made her want to turn to him. To turn *into* him and be held, comforted. But the hand that feathered so lightly over her back, it was hesitant. Not gentle and deliberate the way it had been when he taught her guitar. Not desperate and grasping like it had been that night.

The wisp of air between his hand and her back might have been miles for how isolated she felt. No man was an island, but she was doing her best impression of Greenland—set apart and so damn cold.

"Are you okay?" he asked quietly. "Do you need to see a doctor?"

"Already have." Her words came out clipped, as if she were pissed at him. He didn't deserve that, but she didn't know any other way to be. They weren't in this together. As he'd made clear in the closet before her rushed confession, there wasn't a *together* where they were concerned.

"We need to talk about this. After the lock-in. Will you come over?"

She sighed. Coming over. That was what had started them

down this track. She'd flirted and flirted and flirted—and never really believed anything would happen. For *years*. And then something had changed between them. Slowly first, and then faster, like a train picking up speed. The way he'd looked at her had been more intent, more serious. More sexy in that stern-morality-sex-appeal way.

If you really want to learn to play, I'll teach you. Guitar, he meant. But she'd taught him right back, other things. Grown-up things, because when it came to sex, they were equals.

Not anymore.

Running a hand over her face, she made a sound of frustration. "Can we not do this?"

"Do what?"

"This whole…" She twirled her hand in the air, some vague gesture of futility. "This caring thing. Obviously you aren't interested in being a father. At least, not with me. And that's fine. I don't care."

Liar. And in the church basement too.

"Chloe—"

"I just thought you had a right to know, but look, I'm going to speak to Pastor John on Sunday and quit. You won't even have to see me again. I don't expect anything from you, so don't worry."

At least that last part had been honest. She didn't expect anything from him. She wouldn't do anything to bring him down. It was her choice to keep the baby, and it would be her responsibility.

Except Tim didn't look relieved. No, he seemed…kind of pissed, actually. She wasn't sure she'd ever seen him pissed. His gaze sparked with something like frustration. His soft lips pursed, framed by the scruff of his beard.

He opened his mouth to say something, but footsteps rang

in the gym outside. In a flash she stood and so did he. They backed away from each other, straightening their clothes like two teenagers who'd been caught necking in the bathroom. Only it was the teenagers catching the adults this time. And they hadn't been necking. They'd been doing something much less fun. They'd been saying good-bye. That was how it felt, hollow in her bones.

One of the juniors, Sarah, poked her head inside. "Hey, um, don't freak out or anything, but the popcorn machine is kind of on fire."

"Crap." Tim dug his fingers through his hair like he always did when he was stressed out, only rougher now, faster. He sent her a wild glance she couldn't parse before muttering, "We'll talk later, Chloe. I'm serious."

She just raised an eyebrow.

With a sound of frustration, he left.

Chloe followed more slowly. The popcorn machine did something crazy every time they used it. It was old and broken, like everything else in the church basement. She loved it. She'd miss it all when she left. The crazy popcorn machine, the leak in the ceiling. The kids.

And Tim most of all, more than anything.

The kids were using their pillows to air out the smell of burned popcorn. Tim knelt beside the popcorn machine, muttering under his breath as he banged at the ancient machinery. The man had no idea how hot he looked in the faded blue shirt left unbuttoned over a gray T-shirt. How sexy it was when his too-long hair curled over the collar. How very grabbable his ass looked when the loose denim stretched taut.

Or maybe he did know. The same way she read *Cosmo* and painted her nails the latest color. Maybe he had some sort of youth-leader-image magazine. *Bow ties are* out, it would say.

Lumberjack is in. And thank God for that trend, really, because he rocked this look. Though perhaps her life would be easier right now if he hadn't been so damn appealing.

She clapped her hands. "Come on, kiddos. Grab your sleeping bags, and grab a spot in the gym."

Usually they split the girls and the boys into separate rooms. Then Pastor Tim would sleep with the boys and Chloe would sleep with the girls and everyone's virtue would be safe. But the smell was too strong here, so the boys would have to sleep with the girls tonight.

It would be fine, though. Pastor Tim wouldn't let anything happen. A small smile touched her lips. He wouldn't let anything happen between them either, because he wasn't interested in her anymore. He would probably help her with the baby if she insisted, but she didn't want that. She wanted so much more.

Not going to happen. She was her mother's daughter. She was a cautionary tale. She was a forbidden apple, and he'd already had his bite—but she was the one who would fall from grace.

CHAPTER SIX

LOCK MANAGED NOT to jump the sexy little Sunday school teacher the second her pen left the paper. Her hand had been shaking as she'd signed, and she wasn't ready for sex. At least not the way *he* did sex. So he showed her into the restroom and let her freshen up. Meanwhile he conferred with the concierge to get her bag brought up and her car moved to a VIP spot.

When she emerged from the bathroom, he knew she was ready. He knew by the fresh lipstick on her full lips and the resolved set of her chin. But most of all he knew because of the flicker of curiosity in her eyes. Under the fear, she wanted to know what came next.

He crooked his finger and beckoned her to him.

Her breathing was shallow, her cheeks flushed, and she kept running her fingers through her hair, touching herself. That long blonde hair cascaded around her face in a messy tumble. Bed head, and they hadn't been anywhere near a bed. Wouldn't be near one anytime soon if he had his way. Which he would. This was his show.

She tugged the hem of her short skirt so it covered a sliver more thigh, drew her shoulders back, and crossed the room, steady on her bare feet. She should be plucking daisies, not padding across the plush carpet of his penthouse suite. "Your wish is my command."

No more preamble. If she was really going to do this, he'd know now for sure. "I'm going to fuck you against that window over there, and I'm not going to be *nice* about it. Do you like to hurt, Hailey?"

Her name was a weapon on his lips. A sharp thing he could use to lash her. Every time he said it, he watched her tense. This time she wobbled, her answering nod barely perceptible, her coltish legs giving way under the weight of his regard. And he liked it.

She wanted this thrill, and at the moment finding her sister's baby daddy didn't have much to do with it. Her eyes held wariness and guilt—but most of all, excitement. As if his proposition had jolted her awake. More awake than she'd ever been in her drowsy little East Podunk life, he'd lay money on it.

He'd woken up on stage like that, the whiskey haze parting long enough for fear to creep in, adrenaline spiking into his bloodstream as he fumbled for an instant and then…click. Everything slipping into its proper place. The music. The band. The crowd. All of it more alive, more real, brighter and sharper because he'd come so close to disaster.

Do you like to hurt, Hailey? He'd asked her, and she could only nod.

He'd hurt her so good she'd give voice to that desire before he was through. She knew it. He knew it. The subtext breathed in the air around them, a living thing, that damned contract come to life. *She wants this. She wants the lurid celeb fantasy. The shock, the pulse-pounding vibrancy that only exists on the edge of a bad decision.*

He'd take her there.

"Take off your clothes," he said, a little too harshly, his urgency coming out as hard-edged gruffness.

THREE NIGHTS WITH A ROCK STAR

It didn't scare her away. *She wants that too.* She fingered the button of her cardigan, uncertain, and then popped them all in a rush, exposing a silver tank that dipped low over her cleavage. *Fuck.* Surprisingly lush curves on her willowy frame, and smooth, pale skin.

He shifted in his seat, imagining his cock between her breasts. Making them slick, squeezing them together, and thrusting, thrusting, thrusting until he came all over her neck. Jesus, he hadn't even seen them yet. She put a hand to her throat as if she could read his mind. As if every dirty thought he'd ever had was flashing on his face. And she knew. Why was she taking so fucking long to undress?

Lust propelled him across the room. He grabbed her by the hip and spun her around, pressing his chest to her back. She was warm, soft, every sweet powder-scented inch he could touch. She didn't resist his rough hands skimming under her shirt. She just raised her arms and let him lift it over her head. The silver tank lay discarded at their feet. Next, the bra. *Her favorite part of the day.* He stifled a laugh as he unhooked it, guided the straps down, the blue satin cups slipping free. She sighed into him, letting her head fall back against his chest.

He hooked his thumbs into the waistband of her skirt and her tights and yanked them down to mid-thigh, taking her panties with them. She rewarded him with a sharp inhale, with shock. He stepped back so he could see the top of her ass. A peach, there for the biting. Two years ago he'd have bumped lines off that ass. No. He'd never have gotten near it back then. She'd have run screaming from him in the thick of his addiction. Sobriety had its rewards.

He spun her around again. "All of it off, now."

She pushed everything down to her knees and shimmied it the rest of the way, kicking free of the tangle of denim and netting. The air conditioner purred to life, blasting them both with a burst of cool air. Her nipples tightened to lickable points. When she wrapped her arms around herself, he shook his head, and she dropped them to her sides.

She met his eyes, uncertainty and desire at war on her face.

He gathered her hair in his hand and pushed her against the window wall in his suite, forcing her legs apart with his knee. No one could see in, but the illusion was fucking hot. Her tits smashed, palms flat, breath fogging the glass. His little church mouse on display. The city, all lights and pulsing energy, spread out before them. He never got to see the cities he toured, not up close, just the vistas from his rooms and the blur from a window seat on the jet. He didn't mind so much when he had a hot body between him and the view.

"Do you want me to fuck you like this, from behind, while the whole world watches?" He wanted to bury himself in all her softness. And he wanted it to hurt. Her or himself, he wasn't sure.

Her only answer was the expanding cloud of condensation as she panted. And then she rocked back. The slightest shift, but just enough friction, in just the right place. He ground against her naked ass, his cock throbbing in his jeans.

She turned her head, pressing her flushed cheek to the window, and he couldn't resist running his open mouth up the column of her neck, chasing that frantic pulse, biting the lobe of her ear until she cried out, "Nobody can see."

"Shhhh. Everybody is watching. Let's give them a show." He skimmed over her rib cage, her belly, and lower, until he could feel damp heat. She wasn't wet enough for what he had in mind. Not yet. He wanted to fuck her so hard she'd be bruised. Marked. Damaged. He circled her clit with his thumb, savoring every buck and twitch, and plunged one finger deep.

The slick walls of her cunt clenched tight as he drew back. Almost ready.

"Don't stop," she moaned.

"I'm running things." He bit the sweet spot where shoulder met neck in admonishment, and reached for his belt buckle. Impatient, he yanked off the belt, pulled the condom from his pocket and shucked his pants. All the while keeping one hand tangled in her hair. Holding her in place.

He considered having her put it on him with her mouth, but she probably didn't have that skill set. Though it might be fun to watch her try, to teach her, to corrupt her.

Later.

Sheathed, he positioned himself at her opening, rubbed the head of his cock over her slick folds, and then he thrust. One fluid movement and he was balls-deep in hot, honeyed heaven. Every drop of blood in his body raged toward his hard-on. Fuck. He drew back and thrust again. And again.

God, she felt good, arching to meet him. He gripped her hip so tight his knuckles went white, pulling her back against him as hard as he thrust. He released her hair so he could grab her other hip, get more leverage, and she gasped. How tight had he pulled it?

He wanted to break her, but all she did was bend and bend.

CHICAGO'S JAGGED SKYLINE sprawled in front of Hailey, carving her, scraping her until she felt raw and bloodied. Even the thick-paned window pushed her, *hurt* her, but in a world of cold apathy, the man behind her pulsed hot and…almost caring. Almost loving, the way he stroked her body, worshipped it.

She was reading too much into it; she knew that. The rock star, the player. He could have every woman in the city and already had, maybe.

She was just the novelty item, a punch line he could use back in Vegas. *I fucked a preschool teacher once.* But her body didn't get the joke. Her body was too busy melting in pools of lava at his feet, and what would be left at the end? The volcano didn't care. It burst right down the middle and spilled itself until nothing was left.

The flesh at her sex was oversensitive, abraded despite the liquid pooling there, readying herself, and he knew. His fingers were achingly gentle as they caressed slippery lips. He raised his hand to her mouth, and she opened automatically, her mouth more obedient than her mind. Sandpaper fingers smoothed across her tongue, leaving the musky scent of her own shame in their wake.

Her moan couldn't breach the rushing in her ears, but she felt the sound vibrate in her throat. Felt an answering groan rumble from behind her. Unhearing, unthinking, like animals let loose in the penthouse. *Wild things,* she thought with a voiceless laugh.

A pinch started at the base of her neck, where it met her shoulder. He was *biting* her. With his *teeth.* She gasped. The pain radiated out to her breasts, down her belly, spearing her sex.

"Oh shit." And that she could hear clearly—her voice. Her curse.

"*Yes.* That's right, baby. Let me have it. I knew you were in there in your fucking cardigan. Fuck."

She bucked, moving her hips, rocking heedlessly, uselessly against the unyielding window. Only his body gave, the ridge of arousal twitching and the sleek muscles undulating and the kind man gasping. Strange thought. *He wasn't kind.* Except when he bit her neck and pinched her nipple and her body clenched in helpless surrender, she felt his gift like a benediction.

She fell, through the window and down the rabbit hole. Lost to darkness except for his arms around her, one on her waist and the other teasing the dregs of orgasm from her clit. She shuddered in relief.

Still here. Only three days with him, but she was still here.

His rough grip pulled her back to earth, where she tumbled to the feather-soft bed, drying her sweat and arousal on bleach-white sheets. He didn't join her. Standing at the edge, he pulled her legs up and pressed them apart.

His grin was strained. "We can do better than that, don't you think?"

She barely had time to consider what he meant. Her climax? Had been amazing. The best ever. And he wanted another one, a better one. How were they going to get it? His mouth answered her, pressing against her slippery sex.

Her mind rebelled against the idea. His angular face with its even, neatly groomed layer of scruff. The little tongue piercing that glinted when he said certain words, like *lick* and *slowly*. He was a masculine form of pretty that didn't need to dirty itself in the slick folds down there.

And God, the black eyeliner. Would it smudge? It seemed like a real possibility the way he nuzzled her, unabashedly finding every slick, damp hollow while her hips thrust upward with a mind of their own. Pleasure coiled within her, taking over every impulse.

Her hand fluttered uselessly above the dark crown of his head. What was she doing? Not pushing him, never that. Not holding his head in place. Just frantic, just panicking. Until he grasped her hand and pressed it against the bed—without lifting his head or slowing his torment.

And then he found her clit with a pleasure so sharp it seared her. *His piercing,* she realized, and it did pierce her; it lanced her. That small, smooth ball of silver rained down ecstasy on her weak and untried clit. The previous pleasure blew away like cotton clouds, replaced by a dark storm and a strike of lightning where it hurt the most. She cried out, vague sounds of *ah ahhh ahhh,* and he answered her, groaning, grunting against her aching flesh.

Wild things in commune and she could barely understand. All she had were observations, the tanned curve of his shoulder where it propped up her knee. And things she couldn't see, like how wet she was. She could feel the wetness and hear it.

Too wet.

Embarrassment flushed hot across her skin, and it would only be worse when she came. She wouldn't be conscious enough to guard herself. She'd gush all over his face, and then what? No, no. Her thighs tensed, belly clenched against the impending climax as if she could stop it, as if she had control. A hundred miles per hour toward the edge of a cliff and she slammed on the brakes. And fell right over the edge, tumbled over, headlong. Listening to the echoes of her own shameful cries, sighing in relief as she landed, impossibly light on a plush, pristine surface.

His mouth didn't let up. It just slowed. As if her pleasure hadn't been the goal at all. It was the slippery musk she left on her thighs; that was his prize. He lapped it up, slow and hungry, until every part of her had been cleaned with his tongue. And she, boneless and spread-eagle on the bed, offered him anything, but this was all he took. Only then did she realize, right when he broke the contact, that they'd been holding hands all that time. He finally pushed himself onto the bed and rolled beside her.

She lay like that, drifting. It might have been minutes or hours. Maybe she would have stayed that way forever, except she felt him vibrating next to her. That was the only way to describe it: vibrating. Was he laughing? Crying? Both possibilities seemed horrifying. Her eyes squeezed tight, unable to even watch her humiliation, to find out what she'd done wrong. But on a particular jolt, she had to see. She turned her head, and—

He was touching himself. Stroking himself. When his fist met the base of his cock, the skin peeled back to reveal a curved, glistening head. On the upstroke, he turned his wrist, like twisting the lid off an old-fashioned Coke bottle. He was rough with himself, she realized.

"Can I—" she started. "Do you want me to—" She made a little motion with her hand and her shoulder and hips, not even sure what it was supposed to mean. Was she miming sex now? Was she truly that ridiculous?

"No," he gasped out. And then, as if to make sure she understood, he gave a short, quick shake of his head.

No? Part of her recoiled from the blunt rejection. He didn't *want* her. She'd managed to disappoint him just by having a messy orgasm all over his tongue.

But another part of her was simply confused. Any man, and a famous, sexy rock star at that, didn't lick a girl to orgasm and then just masturbate beside her when he was finished. And that definitely couldn't be normal sex-contract procedure, even if she didn't really know what that would be. He could perform almost any act on her, and the way he was watching her breasts as he touched himself, she knew he wanted to. So why didn't he? A sudden tenderness filled her as she watched sweat bead on his brow.

She brushed it away. "If you want to…do that, it's fine. I'll just help, okay? I'll be right next to you and help."

His lips pursed; his brow furrowed. Even while he fought with himself, his hand didn't stop. He was fighting with himself and jerking himself off, and she wondered if those were the same things.

"Okay," he gasped.

She reached out and paused, uncertain. Her hands hovered above him, like some sort of dirty healer. "What do you want me to do?"

"Touch me," he ground out, still working, still stroking.

She put her palms on his chest. Just placed them flat against bunched, sweaty muscles, an ironing board to unruly wrinkles.

"With your mouth," he grunted, and she leaned forward to place a kiss on a pale brown nipple.

"Lower."

She pressed her lips to his abs. Her eyes met his, and without really planning it, a challenge passed from her to him.

His lids lowered. "Do you want me to make you?"

She could never tell him to do that, not in three days, not in a million years. All she could do was bow her head and pray he would do it anyway. His other hand tangled in her hair, grasped it at the base, and guided her mouth to where they both wanted it to be.

HIS JAW ACHED. His cock ached. Everything ached. She was so much fucking work—exhausting—and he couldn't get enough.

He tugged the silky blonde strands tangled in his fingers and resisted the urge to pull her up to his sticky lips, to bury his face in her hair. Hair that he knew smelled just like the baby powder he sprinkled on his hands before a show.

There was nothing coy about her, nothing calculating. But

she blinked at him with her clear brown eyes, said those *things*, and manipulated him just the same. Maybe if he filled that mouth with his cock, he could break the spell. Maybe he was kidding himself.

She touched him with just the tip of her tongue, tasted him, slipped a bead of precum into her mouth and moaned. A live fucking wire, a shorted-out amp. He felt that flick shoot to his balls, along his spine, right to the top of his head. Jesus. The wet slide of her mouth as she swallowed him was warm and welcome. Slow. She wanted to *help*. It was like his cock found a home.

"That's it, baby. Take it all."

He pushed her down until she made a muffled choking noise, the head of his cock hitting the back of her throat, her lips still not at the base. She didn't balk or pull away; she just relaxed into it. Took it. And then she swirled her goddamn tongue, like a question. He hissed the answer through clenched teeth. "Yesssss."

This was not the plan. The plan was to jerk off with her mouth, use her like a masturbatory sex toy, a living Fleshlight. Fuck her face until she didn't want to look at him.

He wasn't in control anymore.

Spinning on a razor edge of bliss, rocking his hips, he trailed his hand down the side of her face. Caressed her hollowed cheek with his thumb as she worked over him. Her naked body bent to the task, her pale shoulders a stark contrast to his tanned skin. He smoothed her hair back so he could see the gorgeous mess he'd made, her lips pulled tight, her eyes watering.

She smiled.

He let his head sink into the pillows. Let the pleasure claim him, just this once. When her searching hand found his balls, cupped them, that was a question too.

His body answered for him. The orgasm rocked through him like a violent quake. She took it all. He held her there, just to make sure.

CHAPTER SEVEN

Saturday morning

HAILEY STRETCHED, FEELING the warmth of sunlight on her face…and a hairy leg beneath her foot. That brought her up short.

She sat and took stock. A cushy, oversize bed that bore close resemblance to a cloud. An endless view of blue skies through the tall windows. And a rough-hewn man sprawled beside her. She knew there was an explanation for all this. It hovered just beyond her thoughts. But at the moment she couldn't remember the specifics, and right here, this felt like heaven. Or a highly sexualized version of heaven.

The man rolled to face her. Without opening his eyes, his hands reached for her—and found their mark. He pulled her down beside him, wrapping his arms around her, heavy and sweet. "Go back to sleep," he mumbled against her hair, and yes, yes, this had to be heaven.

But then she remembered. Her sister, pregnant. The band, the deadbeat. And the contract, signed.

It was a puzzle, that contract. So formal and yet so…permissive. Like building up walls and then handing her a sledgehammer. Opening her eyes, she saw the side table where he kept the contracts and the lube. Very handy for sudden sex purposes. He'd had a *stack* of them. How many women had signed on the very solid, very puzzling line? Probably lots of them.

He might not even have known it was her. *Go back to sleep* sounded a lot less charming. He didn't want to cuddle; he wanted to hit the SNOOZE button on his human alarm clock.

Gross.

She *felt* gross. She wriggled from his grasp, needing to breathe freely again. He made a grunting sound and tossed and turned briefly before settling back into sleep. He really was pretty this way. Long lashes against tanned cheeks. The heavy eyeliner had faded from his lids, leaving him looking innocent. What a joke. No doubt he had tried everything once and then started over again, like the kinky man's version of *Around the World in Eighty Days.* And she wasn't a Paris or even a Chicago. She was a gas-station stop on Route 66.

She really needed to get out of this room.

At least Lock had the foresight to have her bag brought up last night. She slipped into the bathroom and took a shower, wondering why her skin could still remember the shape of his hands, his mouth, even when pummeled by scalding water. The clothes she'd filched from her sister seemed to fit her even worse today, without the puffery of righteous indignation to fill them out.

A clumsy attempt at makeup completed the disguise.

Hopefully she would blend in. If not, she thought wryly, she could always show them the contract. It was the cool-kids stamp of approval she'd never had back in high school. Of course then she'd owe Lock a bajillion dollars, so probably not. At least she had the little VIP card around her neck, for whatever that was worth.

As she hit the button on the elevator, she realized she wouldn't be able to return to the room without a key card. And

Lock had the key card. Maybe she should wait until he woke up? Nah. She had come here for this purpose. And he'd *said* she had full access to his band and the hotel when he wasn't using her.

Like now.

Downstairs, it looked like most people had cleared out. A cleaning crew had come and gone, leaving the lobby immaculate. No puke by the potted fern. No unconscious guy slumped next to it—she hoped he was okay.

There was one relic from last night, as if to prove it hadn't been a dream. A guy lounged in one of the fancy leather chairs. He was shirtless and shoeless, and his fly was undone. He cradled his head in his hand, clearly worse for the night's partying.

Frowning, she tried to remember the hints her sister had dropped about the guy she liked. *We love the same music.* No surprise there. *He really gets me.* Hailey sighed. *He's just in a weird place with his life right now, and a baby would mess all that up.*

Not much to go on, but hey, she'd found her righteous indignation again. This little road trip hadn't been a well thought out idea. It was pure, unadulterated frustration. Hailey refused to sit around at home and do nothing, and this was all she'd had left. She marched over and plopped herself in the seat across from the guy.

"Hi, I'm Hailey."

He scowled at her. "Why are you shouting?"

"I'm not," she said, but she did lower her voice. "I just wanted to introduce myself, because I'm new around here. You know, to the tour." What did they call themselves? "The group. The...club."

"You don't say," he responded drily.

"But you know, I really love their music. The band's. It's

very…" She had a flash of a dark head wedged between her thighs. "Enthusiastic. And talented."

"So you're here to fuck them." A statement, not a question.

"No." She blushed. Now that she'd signed the contract, it was true. She *was* here to fuck Lock, for three days. Or were they on two and a half now? Something panged in her gut. She should probably find breakfast soon. "Well. Yeah. But I also wondered, since you're part of the band posse—"

"The what?" He snorted.

Maybe not *posse* then. She shook her head. "Doesn't matter. Did you see a girl with the band? Blonde. Young."

He gave her a droll look. "I'm looking at one."

She flushed again. Damn it. "Not me. My…friend. She sold merch for a while."

Should she give Chloe's name? Or flash a photograph? But some old instinct to protect had her speaking in vague terms, protecting her sister's virtue like they were in medieval times or something. Hailey had seen the looks her mother had gotten, even in a town that wasn't small. Reputation was a fragile thing.

He leaned forward, his gaze intent. "Again, I see a lot of girls like that. Girls looking for a good time. I can tell by the dreamy look on your face that someone's already got to you. But you should know, we share. You get bored tonight, come find me. The name's Krist."

She stared at him, unable to move past the two words: *we share*. With a knowing grin, he stood and strolled out of the lobby, whistling something that sounded vaguely familiar.

Hmm. That had gone okay. Not great, though. How was she supposed to figure this out, anyway? Too bad there wasn't a polite way to ask, *So is your life in a weird place right now? Any pressing commitment you can't deal with?* Or maybe just, *Did you have unprotected sex with my sister and then leave her to deal with the consequences, you dirtbag?* But all that was the opposite of subtle.

She didn't have a plan for finding this guy. Nada. Zip. Which sucked, but she couldn't walk away.

She refused to let her sister be publicly shamed any more than was necessary. They'd already had a taste of that in school, when knowledge of their mother's paid "dates" made the cafeteria rounds. The fact that Hailey and Chloe had different fathers, neither of whom they'd ever met, didn't help. Hailey wanted better than that for Chloe *and* her baby, so here she was. Ready to give the father of her niece or nephew a verbal butt kicking. If only she could identify him.

With Krist gone, the lobby was pretty much empty. She doubted the woman with the perfect up-do behind the desk would be interested in spilling band secrets. Wandering through the wide, carpeted halls, she found the bar had opened. Inside, a bartender was wiping glasses as he lined them up, prepping for the day and night to come. He had a metallic blue shirt and an earring, and shadows under his eyes that hinted at late nights. His smile, though, was warm when she sat down.

"What can I get you?" he asked easily.

She immediately liked this guy, immediately felt more comfortable than she'd been recently. "What do you have that's nonalcoholic? And comforting. Like chicken soup. I guess you don't have that."

"Unfortunately not. But I have orange juice, and I can get the kitchen to fix you pancakes. Carbs always make me feel better. What do you say?"

"I'd say you're my new best friend…Sorry, what's your name?"

"Michael. And it's coming right up."

"Bless you."

HE WOKE WITH the top sheet tangled around his neck. Alone. Disoriented. Not as disoriented as when he'd spent his nights in the bottom of a whiskey bottle, but close. The room, unnaturally dark and frigid, hummed with silence. He ran his hand over the empty space beside him. Cool to the touch. She'd been gone for a while, long enough for all that delicious body heat to fade from the soft white sheets. He could have curled around her body and slept for days. Where the fuck was she?

He sat up, fumbled for the phone on the nightstand, and punched the buttons for room service. Before the second ring he hung up. He wasn't hungry, not for food. Maybe she'd been hungry and wandered downstairs looking for a waffle bar, like this was some highway travel lodge.

Lock had figured out young that his parents were icons. What exactly they iconicized had taken longer to figure out— and had alternately shamed and frustrated him after. Krist had been in the same tabloid-frenzied boat. When they'd first formed their band, they had stayed at shit motels, desperate to prove they were more than rock royalty. Struggling to starve so they could be artists. But when they'd signed their first big deal, hiding their parentage had been impossible. He missed the anonymity sometimes, and the waffles. He almost missed sharing a room with his "brother." He'd never been alone back then.

Never had time to think.

A muffled buzz emitted from the nightstand drawer, the one with lube and clean contracts and a freshly inked agreement with Hailey's bubbly signature. He fished the phone out and groaned when he saw a hairy ass on the screen. Fucking Moe.

He couldn't change his pass code fast enough. "You have my pick. What do you want now?"

"You got a sweet little blonde on your payroll?" The smart-ass was damn near giddy and more gossipy than an old lady at the beauty parlor.

"I don't pay them, Moe. That's your deal."

"You know what I mean." And he did. They all did. He didn't discuss his contractual relationships with the guys, but they knew his *situations* were pretty regimented. Especially after that last nuclear disaster had gone viral. And not the kind of viral that required blood work. The kind that couldn't be scrubbed from RedTube no matter how slick the record label's lawyer. He couldn't blame them for thinking he used pros, though no one could confuse Hailey with a professional.

"She causing trouble?" He couldn't imagine what that would even look like. He pictured her trying to lace Krist's combat boots so he wouldn't trip. She'd be crouched on one knee, that too-short skirt riding up, head bent—he coughed. He didn't need a hard-on while he was talking to Moe.

"No, but she's causing a little scene in the bar trying to pay for her breakfast. Won't give 'em a room number."

Shit. All she had to do was give his name. Was his little mouse ashamed? "Are you there? Hand her the phone."

He heard some muffled footsteps and voices as Moe pushed his phone on Hailey.

"Yes?" The sweet tickle of her uncertain voice had him shifting again.

"What do you think you're doing?"

"Paying for my breakfast. Trying, anyway."

"You're mine for three days, Hailey. I take care of what's mine."

"I didn't know your room number." She said it in a fast

whisper. "Do penthouses have room numbers?"

He shouldn't have let her leave on her own. He should've tied her to the bed and fucked her right back into oblivion. Then ordered room service so they could do it all over again after they ate. He'd just been so sleepy, so comfortable wrapped around her. He hadn't slept that well in years. "Just show them your VIP pass and they'll know you're with me. They'll know you're mine. Then get your ass up here so I can take it out in trade."

"Is that how this works? Trade?" She was still whispering, but he could almost hear her smile.

"No. Not really. There is no trade. There's only you giving me your ass."

"Bodily available." It wasn't a question. It was an affirmation. Those two words on her lips, buzzing in his ear, sent all the blood in his head rushing toward his dick.

"Don't make me wait."

"Will there be...consequences?" The quiver in her voice, the hesitation, all thready and breathless, sounded more like anticipation than fear. She just kept surprising him.

"Would you like that?"

She didn't answer with words, only a gasp. A sharp intake that sounded so much like the noise she made when he thrust inside her—he pressed the heel of his palm to his throbbing erection and growled into the phone. "Be here in five minutes, or I'm putting you over my knee."

He hoped she took her time.

CHAPTER EIGHT

TIM TOOK THE steps up to Chloe's apartment two at a time. If he slowed down, he might start thinking again, and if he started thinking, he'd never do what he needed to do. It was early, the sun just peeking over the treetops, but he knew she'd be awake. She was a morning person, and he…had not been able to sleep at all.

He'd never been to her apartment before. The one she shared with Hailey. But he knew where they lived; basically the whole congregation did. They were like pets, the two of them, especially after their mother had skipped town. Food baskets and bags of cast-off sweaters, a few dollars toward a gas bill during a particularly brutal winter.

They'd struggled in ways he could only imagine. He wouldn't add to that. Not any more than he already had. They were going to have a baby. A child who would need food and sweaters and heat and two parents that loved him. Or her. *As long as it's healthy.* That's what people said. The gender didn't matter as long as it was healthy.

He knew what that meant now.

He rapped his knuckles against the door. Would Hailey be home? Did she already know? What would she say? His heart pounded in his chest. That didn't matter either. *Done is done.* It was time to soak up the spilled milk.

Chloe cracked the door, pulling the security chain taut, and peeked out.

He cleared his throat. "You didn't come over."

"Yeah, I thought that was a bad idea. There's nothing left to talk about. We'd only end up hurting each other."

He'd only end up hurting her, is what she meant. But he wouldn't do that. Not again.

"Let me in, Chloe. Just—" He pressed his forehead to the door frame. This wasn't something you did in the communal hallway of an apartment building. Chloe deserved better, romance and flower petals and poetry. He didn't have any of that. All he had were his empty hands and promises. *Not good enough. Not nearly.*

He was thinking again. Thinking was the enemy. "I have something to say, and you need to hear it."

She nodded and pushed the door closed to release the chain.

The apartment was small but clean and cheerful. Hailey had done a good job of making a home for them.

"All right, you're inside. What is it?" She crossed her arms over her chest, and it tented the T-shirt she wore. It reminded him of a baby bump, and he had to clench his hands into fists to keep from reaching out to touch her there. It steeled his resolve.

"Chloe, I don't ever want you to be uncertain or scared or hurt. I know that's how you've felt, and I am so sorry." He reached for her hand, and she didn't pull away. It was tiny compared to his, but strong. He remembered guiding her through the scale on his old acoustic; she'd pushed the pads of her fingers into the strings until they left angry red marks. *You'll callus up if you keep practicing.*

"It's not that—"

"No. Let me talk."

She blew out a breath. "Okay."

"We can fix this. We can make this right. I want to keep you safe, keep our baby safe. Security and family and forever, all of it."

Tears glistened in her eyelashes. "What are you saying?"

He dropped to one knee, still holding her hand. "Marry me, Chloe Miller."

She tugged him up, pulling him into an embrace. "Is that really what you want?"

Cupping her jaw, he skimmed the curve of her cheek with his thumb. "Absolutely."

She leaned into his touch, lips just skimming his as she spoke. "I love you."

Love. This wasn't about love. This was bigger than love. She was confusing lust with love anyway. He'd done the same thing, let his judgment be clouded by base emotions. She'd learn eventually. He'd be what she needed, and what she needed was a rock.

"I'll take care of you."

She stumbled back as if his words repelled her. "What did you say?"

"I'll take care of you. And the…baby. You won't have to be alone."

Hurt flashed through her eyes. "No."

He blinked, confused. "What?"

"I'm not going to marry you."

HE LOOKED SO adorably confused that Chloe almost lost her resolve. Almost gave in to the plea in his eyes. Almost said *yes.*

And wouldn't that be sweet? A husband to take care of her and the baby. *She wouldn't have to be alone.* A fist clenched her heart.

"Is that what I am to you?" she asked quietly. "Someone to take care of? A charity case who showed up on the back step of the church?"

"Chloe—"

"I see what you're doing. You think I'm young. You think I'm stupid."

"I don't think you're stupid."

She laughed. He hadn't denied thinking she was young. Well, she *was.* But neither was she going to be steamrolled by his kindness. It was a form of bondage, that kindness. It would bind their hands together with chains instead of gold bands. That wasn't marriage. It was pity.

"I'm not getting an abortion, if that's what you're worried about."

"I'm not," he said, but something flickered in his eyes. He *had* been worried.

"And you'll be able to see the child. I won't keep you from him. Or her."

His gaze darkened. "So you're making this decision for both of us?"

"I'm making this decision *for myself.* I deserve more than a husband who wants to take care of me." She spat the final words, hating how he'd thrown them in her face. *Right after she confessed she loved him.* "I never had a father growing up. I'm not looking for a replacement."

His head jerked back as if she'd slapped him. "Is that how you see me?"

She ignored the hurt in his eyes. "Tell me it's not like that," she challenged, stepping closer. Her voice dropped as she reached for him. As she backed him against the wall. "Prove it to me."

The hair curling over his collar was silky soft, at odds with the unruly spikes it always formed. She let her fingers slide down his chest. There was so much of him. It wasn't always obvious because he had a way of putting people at ease. *Accommodating,* that was the word. So damn accommodating he froze when she swiped her thumb over his chest, right where his nipple would be. Ah, there it was, hardening so she could swipe it again.

She smiled. "You like that?"

"You know I do," he groaned as his head fell back. "Chloe."

He was always like this, so pliant. Holding back and letting her take the reins. Like when she put her hand on his jeans, and he bucked into her palm. Yeah, he liked that. She knew he did.

"Stop," he gasped.

But she couldn't quite believe him, not with him thrusting in a rhythm she remembered. "You don't want me to stroke your cock?" When he didn't answer, she squeezed. "You don't want me to get on my knees?"

"*Jesus.* Chloe, we can't."

A smile curved her lips. Because okay, this part had always been fun. The denials, the restraint. All the way up until he let everything go. He resisted all the way up until climax—and then he roared with release. His fingers left bruises on her hips, and that was how she knew he'd surrendered.

Not only to her, but to his own lust.

He kept himself back from what he wanted. She couldn't live like that. Not even if she got safety. Not even if she got *him* in return.

She pressed her breasts against him, and God, that was so good. They'd been sensitive lately. She worried it would hurt if they did this again—but no, it felt better. Every nerve ending awake and sparking, a conduit for his heat. Her body slid all the way down his, unbearable friction that drew a grunt from him.

His buckle came apart; his zipper came undone. The hem of his boxers tucked down. It was like tugging on a loose string and watching the whole thing unravel. Him. He was unraveling, leaning back against the wall and letting her take out his cock.

"Prove it," she whispered. Prove he was more than her caretaker. Prove he was more than a youth leader. She needed him to prove she meant more to him than a mistake, something to fix.

She wanted him to love her. But maybe lust would be enough.

His eyes flared as he looked down at her, stroking him in her hands. "Oh God. *Jesus.*"

"What do you want, Pastor Tim?"

"We can't do this. You're…you're pregnant."

"So what? We'll be married but never have sex, is that it?" One stroke. Two. "Do you want me?"

His cheeks were stained pink with arousal. "Yes. Damn it. *Yes.*"

She leaned forward, lips parted, ready to kiss the tip. To suck him deep. He jerked away and nudged her back at the same time. She fell with an *oof* onto her ass, legs splayed. He was turned away, righting himself, straightening his clothes.

When he turned around, the bulge was still clearly visible. Lust strained his expression. But his eyes were veiled. "Marry me."

Too cold to be a question. Too hollow to be a command. What did those two words mean when spoken like that? They meant *duty.*

And she'd already been the albatross around her sister's

neck. She wouldn't also be his. Wouldn't use his money. Wouldn't risk his career plans to become a pastor. Wouldn't face that dead look in his eyes every night when he came home.

She stood, narrowing her eyes and pretending he hadn't hurt her. "Take whatever white horse you rode in on and get the hell out."

CHAPTER NINE

HAILEY HANDED THE phone back to a grinning Moe. He reminded her of Animal from the Muppets, the crazy hair and the whirlwind of energy that surrounded him. It should have been creepy, the way he was sizing her up, like he was actually taking measurements of her body and trying to peer inside her eyes. But somehow it was just sort of inviting, like he *saw* her, and no less flattering because he probably did that for everyone.

"You look familiar," he said, narrowing his eyes.

She shook her head. "I'm sorry. I don't think we've met."

"No, wait. It's coming to me."

She waited, not sure what else to do, especially when he was blocking her way. "Right, well…"

"Judy Garland." He snapped his fingers. "I knew I'd figure it out. You have the bedroom eyes and the husky voice. I'd recognize that voice in my sleep."

She sighed, her fifth-grade Halloween costume coming back to haunt her. With the braids and the blue dress, it was an undeniable likeness. Even grown-up, that hadn't changed. Tripping down the yellow brick road with a tin man on her arm, that was her. She would have preferred to be like someone a little more glamorous. Ginger Rogers, maybe. Hailey doubted Fred Astaire had asked *her* to sign a sex contract.

Or maybe he had. That would be kind of hot.

Moe stepped back. "Come on. Ask Bartender here to close you out."

Bartender assumed an ironic expression at Moe's command. "Room number?" he asked.

"The penthouse, please," she said meekly.

"I'll take you up to his room before His Highness gets impatient," Moe told her as the bartender rang her up.

Too late for that. Lock had sounded very impatient on the phone. Would he really spank her? Her body tightened all over, her skin growing taut, nipples hardening beneath the gauzy fabric of her shirt. She wanted him to spank her.

She'd always wanted that, but she'd never asked her old boyfriends to do it. Because *they* didn't want it, not really, and she couldn't stand for them to think they weren't enough for her. Even if they actually weren't enough for her. It was better to let things drift apart, like wind through a pile of leaves, dismantling them a little at a time until nothing was left. She'd even used Chloe as an excuse. *I'm just in a weird place right now,* she'd said, much like Chloe's missing lover.

The bartender slid a receipt across the ebony bar top, which she quickly filled out with a large tip. Easy to do since it was just a number on a piece of paper, unconnected to her. Like the contract. *Just a piece of paper.* But she knew it meant more than that, or it would by the time Lock was done with her.

Moe had a key card that worked the elevator, and he waved between the doors as they closed her in. Down then up, up then down. Alone again, she leaned her head back against the leather wall tiles, marveling at the topsy-turvy feeling in her stomach.

Was this how it felt to be super rich? Because it was kind of fun, actually, like a trip to the amusement park. She always let

THREE NIGHTS WITH A ROCK STAR

Chloe convince her to do the tallest, fastest ride. She'd clutch the bar for dear life, and her stomach would feel just like this, all turned over and inside out. And in the pictures at the end she'd always have a huge smile on her face.

She raised her fingers to her mouth, just to see. Her lips tingled, extra sensitive, curved into a small smile.

When the elevator doors opened, Hailey stepped into a dark room. Déjà vu assailed her from when she'd come up with Lock. Before she'd had sex with him or signed the contract. Before she even knew who he was. It felt like a lifetime ago, as if that had happened to a much younger version of herself, but that had only been last night.

While she'd been gone, he'd drawn the curtains, blocking out the glossy sunlight she'd seen earlier. Recreating the intimacy they'd already shared. He was in front of her before she realized it, surrounding her before she thought to fight. She was up against the wall, pinned there by him, and she sighed in unexplored relief. A rocky cliff, this relief, only safe from a distance. He ran his mouth down her jaw, along her neck, hurtling her closer to crashing waves. God, how quickly they could turn to sex. The only thing they had was sex.

"You're in trouble," he muttered.

She was gasping, panting. Drowning. "I came straight here."

"Not good enough." He paused suddenly, his body stilling. Only then did she realize how she'd been practically riding his thigh. Good Lord.

Deliberately, as if to make sure she couldn't misunderstand, he grasped her hand and raised it above her head. The other followed, leaving her captive in the bondage of his body, his fingers biting into her wrists. Did he see how much she yearned for that? Did he realize it bound him too?

"Did you find who you were looking for?" he muttered.

She'd talked to some people, but now all she could see was *him*. He filled up her vision and consumed her breath. "Not yet."

"Even if you had, you would have to stay. Three nights."

"One down," she whispered.

"One down," he agreed, nudging hard flesh against her hip. "And when I woke up, you were gone. What was I supposed to do with this?"

He was taunting her. *Testing her,* something whispered inside her. A deep-seated feminine knowledge that knew exactly how to deal with a man in this state, needy and cruel. He wasn't the only one hungry for it. He wasn't the only one who wanted it to hurt. That thick, pulsing erection, probably sticky with precum. What was he supposed to do with it?

"You have a hand," she whispered.

He chuckled darkly. "I'm going to enjoy making you pay for that."

God, she was counting on it.

WITH HER WRISTS trapped under one hand, he was free to explore her body without her fingers asking questions, making demands. He gripped her chin, forcing her to meet his gaze. Her eyes flashed curiosity and heat. She wet her lips, pink tongue darting and retreating, drawing him in. The scent of maple syrup lingering on her breath. She probably tasted like—

No. He wasn't going to kiss her. His goal was torment.

He skimmed the length of her arm, over the top of her breast, down her belly, lingering just below her navel until she rocked against his thigh again. That wet mouth falling open, the damp heat scorching him. Something about her face, the flush in her cheeks, the widening of her eyes—he'd had lap dances that weren't this lewd, this delicious.

"Are you going to, you know, spank me?" She bore down on his thigh, as hard as she could with her body pinned, grinding, finding the friction he was trying to withhold. But her voice was light, like she'd asked him if he was going to make lemonade. If he did, he wouldn't use any sugar. Except he would, for her. If she asked him with that same voice and pressed herself against him when she did.

Her nipples were hard points pushing against the thin fabric of her T-shirt. She'd gone downstairs like that, no bra, tits on display. His tits to play with. He flicked one with his thumb, pinched it between thumb and forefinger and rolled it cruelly. Kept rolling it. She squirmed, arching herself more fully into his hand, sucking that bottom lip into her mouth. He could make her use her mouth again, tie her hands, fuck her face. He could spank her like she so obviously wanted, needed. He could carry her to the bed, spread her legs, and consume her long past the point she begged him to stop. What did he want? He wanted to kiss that syrupy mouth while she jerked and writhed and came all over his leg.

"Fuck it." He let the gravitational pull of her mouth draw him down, let his tongue slip into the space between her lips.

She did taste like syrup. Like waffles. And a home he'd never known. The warm slide of her tongue against his. The soft, sweet swirl of it. It was too much. She tugged against his grip, trying to yank her hands free. Probably so she could draw him down deeper. He didn't let go, wouldn't. He pinned her more tightly. Bit at her lips. Tweaked her nipple harder. Anything to put an edge on this sweet ache. Still she bucked against him, harder and faster. Frantic.

"Oh God." She moaned her orgasm into his mouth. And then she stilled. He'd gotten his wish.

"You're going to pay for that too."

HAILEY SPENT THE final pulses of her orgasm on the hard ridge of his thigh. The soft, worn denim of his jeans was now damp from her excitement, but she couldn't find any embarrassment. Her whole body felt wrung out, sated and soft and impossibly desperate to do it again. He'd flipped a switch inside her with that contract, found the secret sexual part of her and put it on display. She tried to rock against him, to nudge herself toward another peak, but he tightened his hold on her wrists, pulling her up on her toes. He shook his head.

She managed not to say a word she was thinking, not *please* or *more* or *never ever stop,* but he knew anyway. She could see him read them from her eyes, feel the way his cock jerked against her hip in response.

His thigh disappeared from between her legs. His firm hands released her. She was spread lewdly against the wall, and all alone for it. It would have been cold without the fire in his dark gaze, licking its way down her body.

"Here's what's going to happen next," he said. "You're going to walk over to that sofa and bend over the side. You'll flip your skirt up so I can see that tight little ass. And then I'm going to spank you until you're so fucking wet it drips down your leg."

His voice was like crushed granite, washing over her and leaving her skin butter smooth. She could see herself following his directions. She could feel a phantom drop of arousal along the inside of her thigh.

"And when your pussy's nice and wet, all swollen and thick, I'm going to wrap you around my cock and fuck you until I explode."

God. Her body twisted inside, in ways that were no longer pleasure—she was pulsing with something else. With need. The world had gone black-and-white. White was the empty space, the left behind, the sunny smile to hide all her pain. He was inky black, coating her with knowledge and filling her up inside.

"Now," he said.

On shaking limbs made of rubber, she pushed off the wall and walked to the sofa. Its hard angles and shiny leather didn't look inviting, but when she draped herself across the side, it molded to her body. She reached back and flipped her skirt up. The sound he made as he sucked in a breath said he didn't know she'd been bare underneath.

As his footsteps came closer, she pressed her face into the cushion. Her world narrowed to the smell and feel of leather, to the ache of fear in the pit of her stomach. How much would it hurt? Too much?

Or even worse, not enough?

"You went running around the hotel," he asked, "like this?"

The way he said *like this* sounded exactly like *completely naked*.

"No one could tell," she whispered.

He made a sound of disbelief. "This skirt's the size of a dish towel."

"I crossed my legs."

"Jesus," he muttered, and he sounded angry; he really did. But he also sounded awestruck. Almost grateful, especially when he added, "You really wanted this." Like he couldn't believe his luck.

The first brush of his hand over her ass made her jump. He molded the flesh with a possessive touch, a gentle pinch. Blunt fingers probed inward to her slippery folds. She was ready to take him, slick and swollen just like he'd said. But not dripping. He'd made promises when he had her against the wall, and he owed them to her now.

A rush of air was her only warning before his palm landed on her ass. Soft enough to be a warm-up, but hard enough to let her know he wouldn't disappoint. The second came on the other cheek, with slightly more force. He took his time, pulling back and finding a new part of her to abuse. She imagined him watching her skin shudder and turn dark.

"Your ass looks beautiful likes this," he said hoarsely.

Her inner muscles clenched in answer, and as if he heard her, his fingers quested there, searching her out, finding all her secrets. Two fingers circled her clit until she was on the verge of coming. He pulled away. A rush of air, a slap of flesh. There was a rhythm to his madness; of course there was. This rock star who held a stadium of people in his thrall. He could turn anything into music, even the sounds of hurt and longing— especially those.

Every inch between his hand and her flesh wound her up, drew her tight. Every warm flash of pain let her go. She loosened with each blow, with each turn of his fingers around her clit. He never let up, and she never wanted him to. He was sliding his fingers deep inside her, finding a spot that made her writhe on the slick leather, and she was coming apart.

She almost didn't believe the tickle on her leg, how he'd promised her, how he'd delivered. Until he swooped low to lick the trail of arousal, from mid-thigh up to her drenched outer lips, a wet slide along the proof of his words. And at the top he nipped her. She would have shot up then, except for his hand on her lower back.

"Stay still. I need to fuck you now."

He didn't wait to see if she'd comply. A tear of foil and a rustle came from behind as he slipped on a condom. The broad head of his cock sought her entrance. He pushed inside without delay, demanding and greedy. She felt him part the walls of her sex, felt her muscles clench around him.

"That's right. Milk me. Make me spill inside you."

Her body tightened helplessly around him. "Lock?"

He groaned. "Baby."

She wasn't sure what she was asking. All she knew was that they'd almost run out of promises. She'd bent over the couch, and he'd spanked her. He was going to explode, and then what? They were on a speeding train, and she could see the end of the track. Two more days and it would be over. Warm leather caressed her throat as she swallowed.

He rocked inside her, so careful she knew he was close. All he had to do was let go. All she had to do was close her eyes and pray they'd be okay when it was over. She'd never known that sex could be an act of faith, but now that she was here, beneath him, surrounded by him, she couldn't imagine any other way.

He was falling, groaning. He caught himself on the cushion under her, his hand beside her face. His skin glistened in the faint light, sweaty from spanking her, from fucking her. She reached up to grasp his wrist. On a whim, she placed a kiss on the silky skin of his inner arm. He paused behind her, a beat of indecision. A moment of communion.

Then he was wild, pushing inside her—deeper, harder.

She held on tight, to the earth beneath her and the wrist in her grasp, sure she could hold it all together. His grunts were tinged with desperation, like he couldn't get there fast enough. His other hand crushed her hip, holding her down for his invasion.

He came with a rough sound and short, pulsing thrusts. His body felt rigid, levered off her but connected where it counted. In that moment he was purely carnal, a sexual being who'd found completion. She could almost believe that was all it had meant.

Almost, except for the gentle kiss he placed on her temple when he sank back down.

CHAPTER TEN

THE RINGING IN his ears didn't immediately subside. That orgasm had nearly blown the top of his head off. He'd been wound so tight, every slap vibrating up his arm and down to his balls. Pleasure building and building until he had to unzip his pants and fist his cock—squeeze it hard at the base, just to take the edge off—while he worked her over. While he gave her exactly what she wanted, again and again.

And God, the sounds. The smack of flesh against flesh. The rhythm of moan and whimper. The keen when he slipped his fingers into all that wetness.

Lost in those sounds, he'd played her like a song.

He sat on the floor beside the couch, eyes level with her reddened ass, barely able to hear his own thoughts. Just the song. It was so pretty, the melody, and that ass, marked with his handprints. Branded. He reached up to touch his handiwork but hesitated. It would sting. Wasn't that the point? To make it hurt?

Not now. Now he wanted to peel her off the arm of the couch and cradle her. Smooth back her sweat-damp hair. Kiss her temple again. All this sweetness welling up. What was he supposed to do with it?

He'd smacked some asses before, but never like this. Never with such…purpose. He'd wanted to punish her for all the things she'd made him feel. And now that he'd done it, he was feeling even more. Feelings he couldn't even name.

Shit. He shook his head, like that would stop the ringing. If it hurt, so be it.

But it didn't hurt, not if he judged by her soft *mmmm* of pleasure or the way she arched into his touch like a kitten. She'd probably curl up in his lap and sleep if he let her, but they were both too sticky for that.

"Shower." He hadn't meant to say it aloud, but once he did, it felt right. He needed to clean up his mess. And clean up.

"Oh, okay." The sigh she made, so forlorn, nearly undid him.

He stroked over the curve of her calf. "I meant for the both of us. Can you stand?"

He wasn't even sure if *he* could stand.

"Dunno. I'm not feeling very…connected to my body right now. Except for where you're touching me."

"Then I'll have to keep touching you."

He scooped her up and carried her across the room, over the threshold, into the marble-tiled expanse of the bathroom. She was heavy in his arms, a solid weight, despite how small she seemed. Setting her on the edge of the tub, he flicked the water on full blast.

"Not too hot." Her voice was soft, dreamy, disconnected. He didn't know if he should be worried or proud. He thrust his wrist under the jet to test the temperature. Very warm. Exactly how he felt right now.

He lifted her again and helped her step over the tub. She stood under the steamy spray, rivulets of water running down the length of her body, and shivered. "Don't leave."

Usually *needy* pissed him off, but with her it loosened something inside him, untied a knot he didn't know was tangled. He felt so responsible. "Like I said, this is for both of us."

He stepped in behind her and grabbed a bottle of shampoo from the little shelf in the wall and filled his palm. Massaged her scalp with the ginger-scented cream as she leaned into his touch. He worked up a lather, let the soap slide down her neck and over her shoulders. He followed the suds with his hands, trailing fingers over the tips of her nipples, down the curve of her waist and over the rise of her ass. He couldn't stop touching her. Wouldn't. He turned her to face him, letting the water rinse away the last of the soap. Finally she opened her eyes. Clear and bright. "Thank you."

Almost a sigh, that *thank you,* such reverence. It was like a hand around his cock. She grabbed the tiny bottle of shampoo he'd used and soaped up her hands. Her touch was light as she smoothed over his slick skin. Soaped his chest. Her fingernails dragging over his nipples, down the xylophone of his ribs, sending electric bursts of pleasure rocketing under his skin. Jesus, he couldn't think when she was touching him.

He pinned her palms flat against his chest. "I need to get ready for the show tonight. You should dry off."

The look on her face. Pained. *Fuck.* Without thinking, incapable of thinking, just wanting to erase that look, he released her hands, pulled her close and kissed her so hard she'd have a different hurt to worry about. When she softened in his arms, he let her go.

She touched her fingers to her lips and stumbled out of the shower without a word.

By THE TIME she emerged from the bedroom, room service had come and gone. A tray of silver dome caps gleamed by the dining table like some sort of trophy, a reward after very good sex. And seated at the head of the table was the victor, wearing only jeans hanging low on his hips.

She hesitated at the edge of the plush rug. Its thick pile curled over her toes. How could they keep it so white? The robe she wore was white and plush too, everything cloud-like and insubstantial. An image flashed through her mind, a freeze-frame of Julia Roberts wearing a white robe in a hotel room much like this one. Of a lover she hadn't exactly chosen but who'd chosen her. That situation was different, completely different, because a contract wasn't the same as a paycheck. And because there was no fairy-tale ending in her future.

Lock looked up from a notebook he'd been reading. There was a glint in his eye she didn't quite recognize. Not the curiosity from the first night or the lust glaze from this morning. This was...cold. Clinical.

Almost mean.

"Waiting for something?" he asked, and she didn't know the answer, couldn't tell him if she did.

Whatever warmth he'd given her in the shower had evaporated. He'd opened the curtains, and the sun drew his face in bright streaks, remote as a painting. This was him getting ready for a show. This was him pulling away from her. Should she leave? She didn't want to leave.

He raised an eyebrow. "You must be hungry."

She took a step back at the frost in his tone. "I already ate."

"That was breakfast, three hours ago."

Had it really been three hours? She was losing time, losing him. Losing herself, and she wasn't sure where she'd be found again. Outside this hotel, where food was bought with money instead of room numbers? Back home in her two-bedroom apartment, making mac and cheese for supper? But it didn't have anything to do with what she ate or even how she paid for it—that was the problem. The change was inside her, and she wouldn't be able to go back to the way things had been.

His expression softened. "Come here."

She crossed the room, feeling a little silly. It was just a meal. Even rock stars had to eat. Nothing sinister or scary about that. He stood and grabbed a cushion from the sofa. Still not scary. He took her by the hand and led her the rest of the way.

Kind of sweet, actually.

But he didn't pull out a chair for her or even let her go to one. He put the cushion down beside his chair. *Beside* his *chair,* and her mind latched on to that like a clue. Like a footprint dried in the mud, and here she was with a magnifying glass to follow the trail.

The next clue was even more telling—the smoking gun of clues. He slipped the robe off her shoulders, leaving her naked and shivering in the sunlight. He was clothed, wearing a black T-shirt that draped his broad chest. His jeans were also black but faded. Meanwhile she was…naked.

"Lock?"

He pulled the sash from her robe and caught her hands behind her back. He tied them there, using the sash like handcuffs.

Pointing to the cushion, he said, "Kneel."

"What are you doing?" she asked, her voice shaking. He'd ordered her around before. Into the elevator and over the sofa. He had even spanked her butt, and she'd never felt fear. But this, the act of kneeling, somehow seemed scary in a way the other things hadn't been. Maybe because his eyes had burned with lust. And now they were opaque.

He stepped behind her. She could feel the rough hair of his chest on her back. She could feel the abrasive denim against her ass. He completely covered her from behind, leaving the most vulnerable parts of her exposed.

"Just let me serve you, okay?" he murmured in her ear. "It's not going to hurt."

She found herself nodding even though she didn't exactly know what she was agreeing to. He was going to serve her, and his service felt terrifying and sublime. It stripped her to ribbons, but he was at her feet. It left palm-shaped bruises on her ass—but his erection pressed against them, soothing all over again.

If he'd wanted her to deep throat him, she would have been fine. She would have understood. But service? It reminded her of charity and helping hands. And she thought it might hurt after all.

With his guidance she knelt on the cushion, her hands resting at the small of her back. He took his seat in the dining room chair, seeming a thousand feet tall, so far above her. But he could reach down, and he did, holding out a strawberry he'd plucked from a bowl. She stared at the succulent red fruit, wondering why her heart beat wildly in her chest. She'd taken his sex and his pain, his spanking and his coldness, but taking nourishment from his hand felt like too much.

"Open your mouth," he muttered.

He nudged the berry against her lips, and she opened. Sweetness burst on her tongue, and she swallowed thickly, wondering how she could have changed so much, wondering why she felt so at home with a stranger. Did he do this with all the women who signed his contract?

He carefully cut a syrupy pancake and fed her pieces from his fork. He ripped off pieces of a croissant and pushed the torn pastry between her lips. When she was thirsty, he helped her drink from a glass of orange juice, wiping a drop from the corner of her lips.

He looked at her, examining. What did he see?

She swallowed. "Is this what you want?"

A silly question. Of course he wanted it—that was why he'd directed her this way. But the other times it had felt natural to her too, a wild dance that clashed together. This was more like a procession, with him at the fore and her following behind. There was more dominance in his studied contemplation of her than in the thrust of his cock in her mouth.

Her body hummed. Her skin flushed hot and her nipples pebbled under his gaze, even though he mostly looked directly into her eyes. She stared at him too, unable to look away. There were words in those looks, but not the kind she could say out loud. These were messages in a bottle, cast out to sea and found years later, when she'd be ready to have them read.

His erection hadn't ebbed during the meal. It jutted up beneath his jeans, proud and urgent. Her mouth watered to taste him. To drink him down.

He laughed softly. "You're eager, aren't you? But I have to get ready for my show."

It came as a surprise that this wouldn't end in sex. That was the only reason she let loose such a sound of disappointment. And embarrassment too. Without sex, her nakedness just felt…obscene.

He knelt in front of her, lifting her chin with two fingers. His eyes studied hers. "You'll be at the show tonight, won't you?"

She didn't want to go to the show. Didn't want to see a hundred thousand girls throw their panties at him. Didn't want to see him pour his heart out to them in song. But the way he had invited her sounded just like the question *let me serve you, okay?* And though it couldn't have mattered if she came, though *she* couldn't matter to him, she knew he'd be disappointed if she said no.

"I'll be there."

His slow smile was satisfied. "Good."

He untied her hands and rubbed them briskly until the tingles subsided. She dressed in the bedroom, leaving him tapping his pen over ink-smeared notes and lyrics. She had things to do between now and then anyway, people to question. Puzzles to solve, and not just the question of Chloe's lover. There were more questions in her mind, multiplying, dividing. Tripping over themselves until she envied Lock's undivided focus on his notes.

Only when she had gone downstairs did she realize he hadn't eaten a thing.

CHAPTER ELEVEN

STAGE FRIGHT. HE hated it. Hated the sick swirl in his belly. The prickle in his palms. The irrational pound of his pulse. Stupid. He slipped his hand into his pocket, searching by touch for that soothing patch of plastic. His jaw clenched, molars grinding, when he remembered that it wouldn't be there.

"Looking for something?" Moe grinned, a flash of orange wedged between his teeth.

"Give." He held out his hand, and Moe leaned forward like he was going to spit the damn thing into his outstretched palm. He didn't care. He'd take it, if it meant having his pick back before the show. He wasn't superstitious about much, but he'd had that guitar pick in his pocket for every single show since he'd been sober. It had been the only thing left in his possession the morning after rock bottom. The only thing he'd taken with him to rehab. He'd turned it over and over in his fingers during group therapy. During the long, lonely hours when he'd had nothing to do but think about wanting a drink, about never having another drink again, about only not drinking today. There was something about touching it that calmed him, let him step onstage, when for years the only way to get there was to drink half a bottle of Jim Beam. He didn't want to fuck with that kind of luck.

"Just kidding. Only candy." Moe opened his mouth wide for inspection. "Speaking of candy, your girl looks sweet."

He turned to follow his bandmate's leer. And she did look sweet. Standing by the craft services table talking to one of the roadies. Interrogating, probably. She had on a little black dress. Emphasis on little. It stretched tight over her body, revealing every dip and curve. He could just see the outline of her underwear. *Can't have that.*

"We're not done," he growled to Moe without turning back, then stormed his castle.

Of course she was talking to *that* kid. Shit. He didn't want to get sucked into another painfully awkward conversation with Colt. He didn't have the time or the patience for his hero worship. And he didn't have the stomach to sugarcoat some *follow your dreams* bullshit. The last time he'd sent the kid away looking like a kicked puppy. And he'd tried to be kind. Better to ignore him completely. He focused on Hailey, sidled up behind her, gripped her hips and pressed his mouth to her ear. "Am I interrupting something?"

She tensed. "Actually, yes."

Colt blinked in horror, coughing and stammering "I got work" before fleeing. If he'd moved any faster, he'd have left a cartoon dust outline in his wake.

"That was rude. Colt and I were just getting somewhere." He couldn't see her face, but he could hear the pout in her voice, the chide. He wanted to kiss it right out of her mouth. Swallow it.

"I bet." He nudged her forward until he had her pinned against the wall. A position he was starting to recognize as his favorite. He was going to have to mix it up. The last thing he needed were routines where she was concerned. This was temporary.

"You promised I could have access to the crew to ask questions."

He kneaded the flesh of her ass, and she made a noise that was half moan, half yelp. A sharp sound that reminded him she was still sensitive there. Still marked. He squeezed one more time, savoring her squirm, and stepped back. "You made promises too."

She turned to face him, eyes downcast, veiled under heavy lashes, lips wet. "What do you want?"

"Give me your panties."

Her eyes flew open then. "I thought you didn't want me walking around naked."

She squirmed again, hands behind her back, and he knew she was thinking about that spanking. Could only think about that, remember the feel of his palm against her ass. God, was she cupping her own ass? Protecting it? Soothing it? Warming it? It was all he could think about too.

"I want you naked now. That's all that matters. Take them off."

"Here?" She tried to peer around his shoulder, but he had her view blocked with his body.

"I don't like to wait, Hailey."

She sighed, and it wasn't a sigh of frustration. It was a release. His turn to squirm. He shifted his weight, covering the movement with an attempt to widen his stance and shield her body from any prying eyes that might wander by.

She hunched over, bringing her face far too close to his crotch for comfort, and hiked up her skirt. With a shimmy she yanked the panties down her thighs and awkwardly stepped out of them.

"Here." A pant—not from exertion, from excitement. Oh, he could tell she liked this. She thrust a wad of warm cotton into his hand. Lips curved into a sly smile, an unspoken challenge, a saucy *what next?*

He resisted the urge to press them to his face and shoved them into his pocket instead. Not his lucky pick—a new kind of talisman.

"Good girl. Now go sit in the wings. You can talk to anyone here, but you stay put. When we go on, I want you right there."

He pointed to the spot stage right where he needed her, where he'd be able to see her while he performed. He tugged the lanyard around her neck. "With this on, no one will give you a hard time."

"Okay."

Disappointment edged her voice. She tried to step around him, pushing her palms into his chest, but he stopped her. If she wanted shocking, he'd give her fucking shocking.

"Keep your legs crossed, Hailey. Unless..." He hesitated. Would she do it? Could he make her do it?

"Unless?" She stared at his mouth. Waiting. Waiting.

"Unless Krist looks at you." He gripped her ass again, slid his palms down her thighs, and hoisted her up until her legs were wrapped around his waist. Her skirt rucked up to her hips, her naked cunt pressed against his jeans. Not so prim anymore. His lips found her ear, and he trapped the lobe between his teeth. Tugged. She shuddered against him.

He'd forgotten all about his stage fright. "Krist looks at you? I want you to flash him."

HAILEY BIT HER lip. "What?"

"You heard me." His eyes twinkled with mischief. Man, he

was cute like this, all dolled up for his show. His hair was a beautifully arranged mess of midnight blades. His eyes were traced in kohl, reminding her of a pharaoh. That was how he seemed too—like some sort of god, deigning to speak to a mortal like her. He had everyone's attention, the backstage crew casting him glances as they bustled by.

But his attention was only on her.

He raised an eyebrow. "Well? I want to hear you say yes. When I'm out there, I need to know you're going to obey me."

A faint sound escaped her throat. Reluctance? Lust? They two were tied up so tight she couldn't tell the difference. "I want to…to obey you. I just don't know if I can."

He leaned in. "You can. I'm about to go onstage in front of fifty thousand people. Expose myself to them. The least you can do is show yourself to one person. Can't you?"

Her breath sped up. She hated that he sounded so reasonable. It made sense when he whispered low and hoarse in her ear. She'd follow him anywhere, do anything when he cradled her body with his heat. The Pied Piper of sex, and she was drowning.

But he wouldn't be holding her when she was supposed to flash Krist. He wouldn't hold her ever again in two days' time. His hold on her was so temporary it made her ache. If all they had was now, she'd make it count.

"Okay," she breathed. "I'll do it."

He closed his eyes. "Jesus. You don't know what you do to me."

That was when she noticed the slight sheen of sweat across his forehead. At first she thought it was some shimmery makeup, but he seemed jittery too. Was he nervous? She'd just assumed that he'd done this so many times, at even larger venues, that this would be old hat. Apparently not. And feeling nervous, he'd come to her. He hadn't come for her panties, not really. He'd come for comfort, and that she would freely give.

Sliding her hand behind his neck, she tugged him down. And nipped his earlobe for good measure. Comfort disguised as sex, the Trojan horse of bodily interaction.

"You look great." She brushed her lips over his Adam's apple. "How are you feeling?"

"Better now," he rasped.

"I'll be waiting right here, after the show. Ready for you. Wet for you."

His breath caught, and she went to find it, licking along the seam of his lips, darting inside to meet his tongue. *I want you,* she said with her kiss. *I believe in you.* He responded with groan of gratitude.

When he broke away, he pressed his face into the side of her neck and took a long, slow breath in, as if it were a drag and she were the drug. It warmed her in a way that made her want to protect him. It made her want to run and hide, and, torn between the two impulses, she could only remain still, pinned by his smoky gaze.

"Break a leg," she murmured.

He winked, already sliding into character. "You got it, babe."

She watched him stalk away and disappear into the crowd. Man, she had no idea who all these people were. Some of them worked at the stadium, while others followed the tour.

Standing on her tiptoes, she searched the hectic crowd for sight of the guy she'd been talking to before Lock interrupted. His name was Colt something. He worked sound for the band, which meant he had a backstage view of every show. He would have seen Chloe around. He'd know if she was hanging with a specific band member. She'd been just about to ask when Lock

THREE NIGHTS WITH A ROCK STAR

had barged in and scared the guy away. Now she'd lost her informant…and her panties.

Someone rushed past her, sending a breath of cool air up her skirt. God, why was it so short? Chloe was two inches shorter than she was, sure, but even so, this was ridiculous. Keeping her knees together, she slid onto a wooden stool just beside the tall black wings of the stage.

This way she'd be able to see Lock…and he'd be able to see her. All of her, if her legs parted. Did she really want that? A shiver ran down her body and clenched right in that freshly exposed place. Yes, putting on a show for Lock while he put on a show for the world. She could see the appeal.

But that's where her eagerness ended. She'd signed a contract with him and him only. Hadn't she? She wanted him and him only. Not Krist.

Even if Krist did have that tattooed-bad-boy thing going on.

She wasn't into bad boys. She'd always wanted white picket fences and two-point-five kids. She'd wanted to know that her husband would come home every night, that he wouldn't bail, that he wouldn't leave her with nothing but a sperm donation and half a pack of cigarettes. Which was all Lock was really offering her. The donation process might be fun, and whatever the band smoked, it was probably sweeter than Marlboro, but it didn't change the bottom line.

She crossed one foot over the other, undecided about following his orders. She preferred to follow through when she gave her word, but this was…uncharted territory. Panty-less in a public place. Flashing a virtual stranger. She'd tumbled into the wild west of sexual exploration, and she had no choice left but to draw her gun. Figuratively, that is. In reality the only weapon she was packing was far softer, far wetter, and far more dangerous.

The opening act went on, and she lost sight of the guys in Half-Life. She supposed they were together, ready to go on next. The crowd didn't need much warm-up. They clapped in appreciation and clamored for the main act, their energy turning the air electric and raising the hair on her arms.

She hadn't fully understood the scope of Lock's celebrity. She hadn't *wanted* to understand. Why would he be into a girl like her? She knew the answer. He'd spelled that out in the contract: lots of sex and a short fuse. All the benefits of a relationship, but with a ticking time bomb in the middle. And if this awful, inappropriate yearning was any indication, she'd be caught in the blast.

The floor beneath her feet rumbled, the whole building shuddering in anticipation as the opening act left the stage. Lock made his entrance from the other side, and she watched him with a sort of detachment. That sexy saunter and übercon-fident smile—at once familiar and so foreign. It angered her suddenly, this act of his, even as it endeared him to her. She had an act too, with this too-short dress and her pathetic little plan. They were both pretending, both seeking refuge in a game, in a contract, but none of it could make the pain go away. She'd already figured that much out, and she suspected he knew too.

Moe was the drummer, which fit him perfectly, a wild ca-cophony in perfect beat. Lock was on the guitar, and Krist played bass. Unlike Lock, with the single black tattoo on his arm, Krist's body was painted with colors: the blue of the sea, the red of a woman's lips, his skin left bare to fill in the lines of hers.

His body told a story, but then maybe everyone's did. Even Hailey's, with her pale, uninked porcelain. Usually so bland but now…now her ass was bruised. Her skin had pebbled into goose bumps from the cold and excitement. The folds of her sex were slick, endlessly caressed by the air around her.

This was the story she told when Krist turned his head to her at the end of the second song. She met his green gaze, feeling determined and terrified. His eyes widened, a small sign of weakness that soothed her. Not gods after all. Just men. Her knees parted, and for the final act, she lifted the hem of her black dress.

It could have been enough, just that. She'd fulfilled the terms. She'd followed through on her word. Except she finally understood why Lock went onstage even though it scared him. Exposure was a drug, and a single hit left her wanting more. While Krist's eyes burned with heat ten feet away, she slid her finger through her folds, then sucked the wetness off, tasting salt and sex.

His body jerked, nostrils flaring. He missed a beat in the song they were playing; she could tell. Her skirt was down and her legs crossed again by the time Moe sent her a suspicious look. The look Lock gave her a few beats later, though—that was pure pride.

She felt proud too. Her pulse was erratic, her heart racing. Lights danced in front of her eyes, though that may have just been the strobe lights from the rafters. But she'd *done it.* She might be new here, but if this had been the sexual shoot-out at the O. K. Corral, well, she was the last woman standing.

CHAPTER TWELVE

ONE SOUR NOTE humming up his spine and he knew she'd done it. Krist wouldn't fuck up this song they'd played so many times it was burned into their fingers. A sense memory. A reflex. They'd played it in their rented rehearsal space before the band had a name, on the road when they toured out of a beater conversion van, in the studio after they landed a record deal, and onstage for thousands of screaming fans. Their "Free Bird." Their "Stairway." They'd played it drunk and stoned and tripping balls.

And now Lock played it sober, if he could call this dizzy edge of control sobriety. Sweat dripped down his forehead, stinging his eyes, but he just shook it off and kept playing. Thrashing. Ignoring the pyrotechnics, the bright lights. He didn't dare turn to look for her, to see if her legs were still spread.

It shouldn't shake him. He'd already buried his face in that sweet pussy, branded her ass with the palm of his hand, but the idea of her flashing Krist on his command was intoxicating. A dangerous thrill coiled in his belly, warmer than whiskey, hotter than her mouth on his cock.

"I'll lead you down, into the belly of the beast." Their voices merged in a ragged harmony on the chorus. Then heat, as Krist leaned into him. Back to back, all muscle and bone, they pushed against their demons together. Screamed into the night.

"Down. Down. Down." The crowd roared with them.

How far down did she want to go? How far could he go before he couldn't get back?

He turned to face her, but Krist was between them. Of course. His head bent over the slick red bass, fingers working hard, it was almost sexual. No, not almost. It *was* sexual. And sexy as fuck. Lock craned his neck. He needed to see Hailey. Needed to find a center to ground himself, because he was spinning. Not from nerves, not anymore. From excitement.

And then everything stopped. His little church mouse sat right where he'd left her. She pressed her palm to her chest, and it looked like she was trying to slow her own beating heart.

"Let me lead you." He sang alone now. To her. To Krist.

Her mouth fell open. He couldn't hear anything but the music and the crowd, but he could almost feel her panting, feel the warm, sweet brush of her breath against his neck. Her other hand skimmed over her thigh, inched her short skirt even higher.

"Into the belly of the beast." He drew out the last note until it rang like a primal scream as she dipped her fingers between her legs and showed him exactly what she must have shown Krist—only Lock didn't miss a beat. This time she had to know what the words meant. She'd beg him to take her there before the night ended. Maybe he'd make her beg Krist too.

He stormed offstage, tossing his guitar to a roadie before he reached her.

"That was amazing." Her eyes were wide, pupils blown. Probably with adrenaline and lust.

"What? The set? The flash?" He pushed her knees apart and forced himself between her legs.

"All of it." She let her head fall against his chest, and now he really could feel her breath, cool against his overheated skin. She clawed his sweaty back. His pulse stuttered.

"Do you want him?" She had to know he meant Krist.

"I want you. I want what you want." She pressed a kiss to his pec, right over his heart.

He'd have to figure that out. What he wanted. Soon.

"That's good, baby. Now, keep your knees together for the rest of the show."

"And if I don't?"

Her wicked grin, all sin on an angel's face, grabbed him by the balls. All he could do was kiss it off, slant his mouth over hers and swallow that smile, trap her bottom lip between his teeth with a sharp nip. "I think you know, but I'll be forced to get more creative."

A roadie coughed beside them, vibrating with anxiety as he cradled Lock's Fender. He retrieved his guitar and jumped back onstage, his fear barely an echo.

HAILEY'S ANXIETY ROSE along with the intensity of the concert. By the time it crescendoed with a blaze of pyrotechnics and a roaring crowd, she was an electric mass of nerves. Lock wouldn't really share her, would he? When Krist had claimed so, she'd assumed it was bravado. Even when Lock ordered her to flash his bandmate, she'd assumed that would be the end of it.

But those assumptions had been willful naïveté, those of an ostrich with her head stuck in the sand of inexperience. The reality was something far racier. The reality was that most of the women in this impromptu backstage after-party were wearing fewer clothes than she was, and considering her short-short dress, that was saying something.

The reality was…exciting.

But also scary. Was she really ready to be shared? At least she knew Krist, a little bit. At least she found him attractive, with his colorful tats and perpetual sardonic expression.

Maybe it would be scarier to *do* the sharing. To watch Lock with one of these women. As much as she knew she didn't have a hold on him, as much as she pretended not to care about that, she wasn't sure she could watch him with someone else. To see him get hard for someone else, to watch him spank another girl's ass and then invade another girl's mouth while Hailey sat on the sidelines? It might be the straw that broke the three-day contract's back.

Lock's agent grabbed him as soon as he was offstage, for photos and a brief interview with the press. Lock looked haggard and faintly harassed, but no one else seemed to mind. The agent barked orders, and the fans smiled up at Lock adoringly. Was she the only one who could see the tension bracketing Lock's mouth? His smile looked rigid, the very opposite of happiness, but the press ate it up, snapping pictures, blinding him with their flashes and a spray of questions. Just as quickly Lock's agent yanked him away, freeing him from the horde and forcing them back.

She watched Lock scan the crowd. His gaze zeroed in on her. *Oh damn.* He looked intense. Angry. Not mad at her, exactly, just fierce enough to raze anything in his path. Which would be her. Only her. Everyone else was smart enough to duck away as he crossed the black, springy flooring. She remained rooted to the spot, waving a red flag in the form of her short-short dress. She'd already figured out he liked her legs, and no amount of tugging on the skirt covered them up.

His skin shone with sweat. He was still breathing hard,

making the illusion of him as a bull come to life.

She knew she was staring. She had no way to stop. "Hi."

"Limo," he barked.

"What?"

He bit out the words. "Get in it."

She glanced behind her. The chauffer who had brought them stood holding open the metal backstage VIP door. "Oh!"

Lock didn't waste any more time. He herded her through the remaining crowd, out the door, and into the limo while she struggled to remain upright in her tall shoes. Then she wasn't upright anymore; she was held up by plush, butter-soft leather. The driver closed the door, instantly dimming the volume. Sudden intimacy bloomed between them, with Lock's breath ragged and loud in the car.

As the driver rounded the limo, Lock dragged her onto his lap, arranging her so her legs straddled his. She knew the windows were tinted. The fans and press couldn't see them anymore. Most likely the driver wouldn't be able to see them either, and if he did, he would be professional enough not to comment on it. Still, she squirmed until Lock slapped her thigh.

"Be still."

She looked him in the eye, keeping her balance under the incremental motion of the vehicle. So they weren't going to be sharing, either one of them. Good. That was good. She shouldn't feel disappointed.

The limo began to roll forward—then there was a quick banging on the roof of the car. Startled, she almost fell off Lock's lap until he caught her in his firm grip. Was it one of his fans? Or a member of the press? The pushy agent?

The door opened, and she shrank back into the warmth and safety of Lock's arms. It was Krist. He slid into the opposite seat and shut the door behind him. The limo started again when he banged on the divider, and then sped up as it turned onto the main road.

Krist. In the limo with them. While she was straddling Lock's lap.

"*Lock.*" She struggled to get off, but he smacked her thigh again.

"I said be still. Do I need to tie you down, or are you going to be good?"

It was on the tip of her tongue to ask how he would tie her down in a limo. But he probably *did* have a way. And she wasn't keen for him to demonstrate in front of Krist, to give Krist any more of a show than he was already getting. He slouched in his corner. The shadows almost obscured him, but looking back, she could see his eyes shining. Could see them trained directly on her ass.

As if confirming, Lock murmured, "Krist's always been an ass man." Then to Krist, "Haven't you?"

"Fuck," Krist answered, not taking his gaze off her. Not taking his gaze off her ass, technically. It was embarrassing. And hot. Like really hot, with her body all flushed and sweating.

"You don't mind if he's here, do you?" Lock asked while sliding his hands up her thighs.

She whimpered, because God, how could she mind anything when he caressed her like that, when a million pleasurable needles sank into her skin everywhere he touched. She felt her mind fogging, growing hazy and lax in its newfound need. She couldn't stop this, couldn't bring herself to mind Krist's quiet communion.

Not even when Lock's hands cupped her ass. Under her skirt.

At least Krist couldn't really see. If anything, Lock's hands were another layer of protection. Her skirt. His hands. A living chastity belt keeping her safe from prying eyes.

"So good," Lock grunted. "You feel so good."

He proceeded to demonstrate the *feeling* and the *good* as he massaged her. More firmly, more roughly until she was rolling into his touch, rocking herself on the ridge beneath his jeans. And when she felt a brush of cool air against her slick folds, she knew. He was lifting her skirt. He was doing it on purpose. She glanced back. Krist had slouched down even farther. But his eyes weren't on her ass. They weren't on her face, either. They were staring straight at Lock, filled with something like jealousy.

Krist's gaze flickered back to her ass and what Lock was doing to her. Now she saw only appreciation and lust. She could have imagined the jealousy, the *want*. But she hadn't. Krist had made it plain he liked her body, but he had no claims on her, no desire to make any. Jealousy didn't make any sense. Unless…

Unless Krist wanted Lock.

Suddenly sharing Lock took on a wholly different meaning. It wouldn't be some nameless fan girl backstage he'd be spanking or fucking. It would be his bandmate, his friend. Lock didn't seem to notice Krist's appreciation. He licked at the hollow of her neck, and she gasped, overwhelmed. Her body was on sensory overload, but that was nothing compared to her mind. A million dirty images blazed a trail of sensual discovery. And below that, she had questions about these men she'd only recently met. Did Lock know? Did he care?

And even deeper, in a place she dared not dwell, a dark beat drummed. *Mine. Lock is mine.*

Lock must have felt her distraction. He lifted her chin until she met his eyes.

"Are you up for this?"

"Up for what?" she asked, stalling.

"Anything. Everything."

Sharing. That's what he meant, and she was up for it. Only, it was less clear that everyone would get what they wanted. She wanted Lock, to really have him, possess him if only for a night. If she wasn't mistaken, Krist wanted that too. Except Lock was the man in the charge. He gave the orders. And he blazed like a molten comet across the dark sky, too hot and too damn fast to ever hope to catch.

"Yes," she answered in a low voice.

"Hey." He kissed her on the lips, closed-mouthed and quick and achingly sweet. "Don't worry. This is going to be fun. You know I can make it good for you. Krist too."

This last was spoken with invitation, waiting for Krist to speak up with the reassurance that it would be good for her, that she would get off. As if that was the reason she would hesitate.

Krist leaned forward, out of the shadows. Whatever secrets he'd exposed were wrapped up tight, leaving only genuine concern.

"Only if you want to," he told her.

She mourned how he stayed on the perimeter, on the outside looking in. She no longer liked where she sat, in between them. She didn't want to get in their way. But if she could, if they needed her, she could be the bridge between them.

"Sit with us," she said simply. These waters might be stormy and dangerous, but they would ride them together. She would hold their hands tightly and link them, if only for one night.

CHAPTER THIRTEEN

*T*HAT WAS AN *invitation, right?* Krist had yanked him close to hiss the quick question into his ear before they were herded like cattle to VIP photo ops and bullshit PR.

Was it an invitation? He'd intended it more as a taunt, but something had shifted onstage. Had maybe started shifting long before he took the stage, before he'd given Hailey that crazy command. He'd told Krist to meet him at the limo. *You drinking again?* That question stung. But it was valid. They'd never shared sober. No, *Lock* had never shared sober.

And Krist had never shared with anyone but him, which might explain the hungry and hopeful edge to his voice. It'd been a long time.

Only if you want to. Tender. Considerate. All the things Lock wasn't. And traits he hadn't associated with Krist before now. Was this new, or had he been paying piss-poor attention?

If Hailey said no, it ended. Contract or not. Krist would slump back against the plush leather seat and watch from a distance.

But she didn't say no. And now he was beside them, all hot muscle, practically vibrating with eagerness. An animal ready to pounce as soon as the cage door snapped open.

Hailey lifted her hand from his shoulder and reached for

Krist. The contrast of her pale fingers against the riot of color on the bassist's forearm was shocking. Lock squeezed her ass. "Did I say you could touch him?"

She pulled her hand back fast, as if suddenly the inked flames licking up that sinewy arm were real. Her brow furrowed, and he fought the urge to smooth it with his thumb. "I thought that's what you wanted."

He did want. He wanted so much. God, he was going to fuck this up before it even got started. "I do, but I'll tell you when to touch him. Right now he's going to watch you come in my lap before we get to the hotel. Better hurry."

She didn't move. Just sat there, studying his face with those doe eyes. "You want me to…?"

"Get yourself off, Hailey." He thrust up as he pulled down on her hips, pressing the ridge of his cock against her bared cunt. She arched into it, gasping.

"And if you're very good, I'll let him help." He released her hips, leaned back and folded his arms behind his head. Calm. In charge.

He thought she'd grind against his leg, like she had at the hotel, rock herself to a quick orgasm against the rough denim covering his thigh. He'd thought wrong. She rose up on her knees, grabbed the hem of her dress, pulled it over her head and dropped it in Krist's lap. A scrap of shimmery fabric to hide the erection that had to be building. She cupped her breasts, skimmed over her belly and hesitated just above the slick center he knew she ached to touch. He knew because he ached to touch it too.

He'd told her to put on a show, and he was learning that she was very good at doing as instructed. She dipped one finger between her lips and swirled it over her clit, slowly, deliberately. A challenge. Call and response.

The bench seat bounced as Krist inched closer, lured by the hypnotic roll of her hips. She wasn't even moving her hand anymore, just bucking against it. Her head fell back, and she was the perfect picture of abandon. Writhing, bent, spread open. Every soft inch of her body screaming *touch me!* Begging. "Please. Please."

Yes, please. He wasn't sure if he was doing this for her or for himself. He traced the hollow of her throat where he'd licked earlier. "She's so sweet, right here."

"Yeah?" Krist's breath huffed warm against his ear and cheek. If he turned, their lips would be touching. He licked his own lips and swallowed, suddenly aware of the tightness of his pants, the dryness of his mouth, the smallness of the limo seat.

"See for yourself."

Krist slid closer, threading one arm behind Lock until they were practically cuddled against each other, and extended the other so he could cup Hailey's jaw. "May I?"

She nodded and settled back into Lock's lap so Krist could reach.

That mouth working over her neck. Wet tongue, flicking. He had a front-row seat, and he couldn't help but imagine all the other places he'd like to make Krist taste. On her body. On his own. She gasped when Krist nipped at her jaw. The two of them were warm and solid, pinning Lock in place.

How fucking long did it take to get back to the hotel? They needed room to maneuver.

"Need to come." Lock's grunted command was almost an admission. But neither Hailey nor Krist could see his state right now, both of them with their eyes squeezed shut, focused on their own pleasure. Krist had a handful of her breast, her nipple trapped between his thumb and pointer finger.

She moaned in response, and he could hear the wet sound

of her hand working faster between her legs. Her knuckles rubbed against his cock on every thrust. Just enough friction to keep him on edge. If they kept this up much longer, he'd come in his pants.

Krist caressed down her ribs and covered her hand with his own. Lock watched, riveted. And then it was Krist's knuckles grazing his cock over and over.

Hailey pulled her hand free, letting Krist finish what she'd started, and traced over Lock's lips with her wetness. He bucked up into those broad knuckles and sucked her fingers into his mouth. The taste of her. The sound of her moans, building and building. The feel of Krist, around his shoulders, against his cock. It was all too much. Krist's eyes were open now, but he wasn't watching his hand slide in and out or her face breaking with ecstasy. He stared at Lock. His eyes were dark with lust and soft with relief. Wary too. Unspoken communication passed between them like it did onstage, like it had when they were teenagers. *Don't make me stop. I won't stop, not now.*

When she finally came in his lap, gripping his chin, shuddering and grinding Krist's hand into his crotch, he came too. Hot and shameful.

How could he walk to the elevator like this?

In the dim light of the limo, all he could see were shadows and flashes of skin, the dip of her waist, the peak of a nipple. Tempted, on edge, he leaned forward and caught it between his teeth. Tugged until she whimpered. Pushed herself forward into his mouth. One flick of his tongue and he released her. "Krist, hand over her dress."

"Suuure." Krist's voice was syrup slow. A low rumble vibrating against his neck, down his back. All reverb, no treble. He watched as Krist untangled his fingers from between their legs and wiped them on the front of Lock's shirt.

The fucker. Lock caught Krist's wrist and pinned it against his chest. "You made a mess."

"I didn't think you'd mind." Krist tried to pull away, but not very hard. It was almost as if he was pulling just so Lock would hold him tighter, longer, like one of those Chinese finger traps.

"I don't just mean this. I didn't tell you to make me come."

"Not my fault if you don't have the control you—"

He squeezed Krist's wrist, his knuckles going white with the effort, and the bastard smiled. "Wrong. You're both to blame," Lock hissed.

"We'll make it up to you." Hailey's hands were soft against his, smoothing his fingers, gentling his touch as the limo rolled to a stop. He let go. So they were a *we* now? A team?

"Get dressed." He'd like to make her walk naked from the car, through the back entrance of the hotel and straight into the elevator. Show her, show Krist exactly who she belonged to. They weren't going to fight over her like a piece of candy. He was going to let Krist taste his candy and then take it away. *Mine.* His cock twitched at the thought. But the fucking paparazzi was probably camped out in shrubs, hanging from drainpipes. Vultures. Vermin. He urged her off his lap, smoothing her hair away from her face as she wobbled onto the seat across from him.

Krist made sure she was covered before he knocked on the window to let the driver know they were ready. "I'll head up first. Meet you upstairs?"

He was running this show, not Krist. "You'll wait in the fucking elevator."

"Got it." The driver opened the door, and Krist tumbled out into the night. Hailey started after him. Lock hooked an arm around her waist and pulled her back into his lap. She gasped, breasts heaving above his arm.

"Wait. If anyone's out there watching, they'll get tied up with him. Give it a minute."

"You don't want anyone to see us together?" She squirmed, trying to turn and face him, the soft curve of her ass grinding against his sticky crotch. Reminding him.

"I don't care what they see. It's not what they see that's the problem. I don't want to give them a piece of us. To use. To twist." He skimmed his hand up her chest, her neck, catching her chin. "I'll share you with Krist, tonight. But only him." *And only tonight.* Their time was almost up.

She relaxed into him, her back pressed to his chest. He could feel his heart pounding against her. More reverb. "We could just stay here, couldn't we? Tell the driver to go around the block a few times?"

"You changing your mind about all this?" He dragged his teeth over the nape of her neck. So sweet.

"No. Are you?"

"I never change my mind."

He tucked Hailey under his arm and led her into the hotel.

Krist bounced in the corner of the mirrored elevator, arms resting on the handrail that ran around the middle of the box. He pushed off when he saw them, so that he stood in the center of the car. "Jesus, I thought you weren't coming."

"But you didn't leave."

He nodded, eyes downcast. "You told me to wait."

Lock pressed the button to close the doors, and swiped his card for the penthouse. As soon as the doors snicked shut, he flicked open his jeans. "Take the dress back off, Hailey. You two are going to clean up this mess you made before we get upstairs."

His cock was only semihard now, but as soon as he felt their eyes on him, it stiffened farther. The car lurched up, and he steadied himself with a hand on Hailey's bare shoulder. She dropped to her knees, curling one arm around his thigh and pressing her cheek against the front of his pants. "Whatever you need."

Krist took a step forward and dropped to his knees too. He dug his fingers into the waistband of Lock's pants and tugged. Hailey pulled away so she could help. His cock sprang free, and he tilted his hips, watched them work in the mirror. Krist's broad shoulders and dark head next to Hailey's blonde waves and narrow back. An angel and a demon. He hissed. Both with mouths like sin.

He didn't look down, not yet. He knew her tongue, a warm dart against the head of his cock. A flick. Krist's was wide and wet, sliding up the length of his shaft. Fuck. When Krist and Hailey tangled tongues at the tip, both working the same sensitive spot, pleasure coiling deep in his balls, he cupped Krist's head and pushed him down. Letting her watch. He looked then. Her mouth open, lips slick, riveted by the sight of Krist bobbing up and down on his cock. She squeezed his ass, pushing him farther into Krist's mouth. Bossy.

He hissed again. He wouldn't come this time. Not for a while. "Enough."

The door dinged open behind him. The suite, cool and dark, reflected in the mirror. An empty bed, waiting to be filled.

HAILEY STUMBLED INTO the hotel suite, the pointy heels of her shoes tilting sideways in the plush carpet. She'd already had an orgasm in the limo. She'd tasted Lock's come, cooling on his skin. But instead of feeling sated, she felt strung up, like a live wire in the puddle that was Krist's unfulfilled desire.

Lock's clothes were already undone, and he shrugged out of them now, the soft leather and torn cotton sloughing from his body like water. His cock was already hard again, standing proudly from the cloud of black hair at the base. Lock was accustomed to standing in the limelight. He did it now, basking in her appreciation. While Krist waited patiently. How long had he waited? Longer than this night.

Fair play. Everyone gets a turn. These were rules Hailey taught in class, but how could she if she didn't follow them herself?

It wasn't only logic that drew her to Krist. With his colorful skin and eyes filled with longing, he made a sexy sight. Soulful.

"Get on the bed," she murmured.

His eyes widened. He glanced at Lock, who watched back with a hooded look. No reprieve there. No answers. He could take what she gave him or get nothing at all.

Krist slunk to the bedroom, looking sullen, resentful. She could have believed it, almost. Except for his obedience, in a man born to rebel. Every hard line of his body promised defiance, but with Lock he was submissive. Borderline meek.

With her too. And it turned her on to see him that way. To see him follow her order and then wait. Her sex clenched in undefined need, but which man could fulfill her, the one raising his eyebrow in challenge or the one waiting on the bed? She knew the answer to that question, at least. The man who gave her every single thing she'd never been able to ask for. The one who took all the things she'd wanted to give.

But tonight wasn't about her. It wasn't even about Lock.

She followed Krist into the bedroom and climbed onto the high, plush bedding. It felt like kneeling on a cloud between his legs. He stared at her, waiting. Anger flashed in his eyes, sweet and vulnerable. Did he know how much he gave away with every taunting phrase or bitter smile? Even Lock didn't know. He poured his heart into his songs and called it an act. He claimed her, body and soul, and called it a contract.

No, they didn't know. Even she didn't, really. They, all of them, saw what they wanted to see, and in Krist's waiting body, she found her reprieve.

She tugged at the hem of his distressed jeans. "Take these off."

His gaze went to Lock again, over her shoulder. Hailey felt his presence, knew he'd followed her into the room. Whatever look he gave Krist must have been assent, because the jeans came off. Nothing underneath. Nothing but bare bronzed skin sprinkled with dark brown hair, startling without a drop of ink. His feet had words twined around them, the y's and f's jutting out like thorns on a vine. But the long shins and rectangle bone of his knee, they were bare. And the furred thighs were bare too…and there. Smooth purple skin underlaid with veins. That had never been touched by a needle. Without the colorful tattoos she was used to on him, he looked far more naked. Far more innocent.

Closer to her level, and it was a relief after looking up at Lock these past days.

She skated her palms along the insides of his legs, enjoying his sharp intake of breath. She framed the base of his cock with her hands. It bobbed gently. The tip glistened, wet and needy. This, at least, she understood. There were no clauses to read, no bottom line to sign. Just a man in his need. Open. Honest.

And only possible because Lock stood behind her. Because he'd orchestrated this entire thing, and that made it okay. It pissed her off to think she was that dependent on him. And yet it was only when his fingers stroked the back of her neck that she bent to kiss the crown of Krist's cock. Only when Lock's fingers tangled in her hair and pressed her down did she swallow more of the pulsing length.

Lock's voice rumbled against her ear. "God, he needs it, doesn't he? Can you feel it? Touch him and see how much he needs this."

Only then did she cup the tender sac beneath his erection, velvet-soft skin pulled taut. Krist's body jerked at her touch. He let out a groan that filled the space around her, wispy air while she still had Lock to ground her.

She set a pace to please him, to give him peace, and Lock muttered his approval. Krist was close; she could tell by the harsh salty flavor of his precum coating her tongue, by the small, urgent thrusts of his hips. Lock's hand left her neck, and she mourned the loss of him, the heat. He leaned over Krist instead, tracing thick black lines on his chest.

Krist's eyes fell shut on a moan so heavy with need she didn't know how Lock couldn't hear it. Though maybe he did hear it then. Maybe he'd always heard it, because he didn't act surprised. He looked solemn, really. Accepting, as he walked his fingers up Krist's chest. As he slipped two fingers inside Krist's mouth and watched him suck.

Krist's hands clenched and opened on the bed, spastic and uneven. On any other man, with a mouth on his cock, he would have been holding back from grabbing. From thrusting. But not this time. This time it was Lock he wanted to grab, and she knew that because she wanted to grab Lock too. She wanted to press her hand to the back of his neck and push him down—the same way he'd done for her. To make him do what he really wanted.

Neither of them needed to force the issue. Lock was ready.

For this, at least, Lock was willing. He pried Krist's mouth open with those two fingers and bent to kiss him. Though *kiss* may have been the wrong word. It was more like an assault, an invasion, and Krist's whole body strung up tight to receive him. His cock pulsed in her mouth, preparing her.

On impulse she slid a finger beneath his rounded flesh, down to the pucker beneath. Between the tongue in his mouth and the finger pressing against his asshole, it was too much for Krist. He bucked and exploded on her tongue. She swallowed the warm come he sprayed in her mouth, and pressed more firmly until warmth hugged her fingertip.

He seemed to go on forever that way, gasping into Lock's mouth and coming into hers. Or maybe it only felt that way as she watched them kiss, his desperation and Lock's gratification. Lopsided and bittersweet. It was how she must look with Lock too, and so, when Krist finished, she licked his softening cock gently, thoroughly, until he was clean. She rested her cheek against his thigh and closed her eyes.

Because she knew exactly how it felt to want something you couldn't have. There was no fair play for love, just for sex. And everyone might get a turn, but no one could keep Lock if he didn't want to stay.

CHAPTER FOURTEEN

THE ROUGH STUBBLE surrounding Krist's mouth abraded Lock's lips, but he didn't care. He liked it. The burn and then the slick heat of tongue, soothing. The guttural moans vibrating against the hand he'd splayed against Krist's chest. Lock dug his fingernails into the swirling lines there, like he could wring a note from this beautiful body that would smooth out the discord in his head.

Want. Take. He'd lived his life that way for so long, until it almost killed him. Until all his wanting turned bottomless and all he could do was drink and take and fuck everyone else. He'd never stop wanting, but the taking had stopped. He had control now. Only, nothing about the feel of Krist writhing beneath him felt controlled. It felt wild and reckless. And inevitable. A rock slide of lust and need. Hailey's muffled hum of pleasure chipped away at the last guardrail.

She lay spent and naked. Sprawled over Krist's long leg, her cheek resting against his hip, watching him. Every soft inch of her, an invitation to destruction. A body made for giving.

"Come up here."

She pushed onto her hands and knees, crawled to the head of the bed, knelt beside Krist's shoulder and waited.

"Do you know what he needs now?" He wondered if she'd go there. If she could take both of them at the same time. He wanted the tight grip of her ass, Krist buried deep in her cunt. He shifted on the bed, the phantom drag of knuckles through denim making his cock pulse.

She skimmed her fingers down his arm and covered his hand with her own. Held it down, over Krist's thundering heart. "He needs you."

He sucked in a breath, gut punched. He'd known, but it had never been said out loud. So simply, so plainly. Krist turned his face into the pillow, trying and failing to hide the look of longing. The desperate want. Lock couldn't ignore it; it was so much like his own.

Would it break them, to do this? Break him? No contract. No plan. Just taking.

Hailey squeezed his hand again and then brushed her fingers over Krist's cheek. He leaned into her touch, and their eyes met. It was like writing a song together, this connection. Fumbling toward the chorus, a jumble of noise, and then yes, of course, music. Loud and violent, but theirs. Hailey smoothing the harsh edges. A bridge.

He'd loved Krist for what felt like his whole life. He could give him this.

HAILEY RAN HER fingers down Lock's forearm, light touches meant to soothe. He was coming apart right in front of her. She knew how to reach him, though, with some ancient instinct. It wasn't even a woman to a man. It was a light in the dark, water running over rock until it lost its jagged edge. She was the water here—the fluid, transient thing. The one who would be gone soon enough.

But Lock, God. He was a rock, from the tension of his

body and the clench of his jaw. And the impenetrable walls he'd built around him, falling down, crumbling.

"You want both of us?" Lock asked tightly. At the same time, he meant. The shadowed space between them. Those jagged edges come to life.

"Yes," she whispered.

A black eyebrow rose, shining onyx in the dark. "Are you sure? You sound afraid."

Said the Pied Piper to his subjects.

But she wasn't afraid, not really. This was what she'd signed up for. This was *why* she'd come, at least partly. To experience the wild, crazy things she'd never done before. To ignore the responsibility to her sister for three days. No, not afraid. She looked over the inky waters and wanted to drown.

"I can handle you. Both of you." Her voice was low and throaty, the song of a seductress. That was what he'd made of her. A siren. A mermaid, and only when he dragged her under would she finally be able to breathe.

"Turn around." He twisted his fingers to show her. "Put your back against Krist. Let him support you."

Let him support you. Because Lock wouldn't.

Krist scooted against the headboard, unashamed in his nakedness. His muscled legs sprawled open across the rumpled bedsheets, dark against light. He was a picture of indolent relaxation, of sumptuous invitation, and she would have believed it. Would have, if she hadn't reclined against him and felt the rat-a-tat-tat of his heart. A machine gun in his chest, the prelude to devastation.

His cock was thick against the small of her back, nudging insistently with a wet, scribbled line. But that was nothing new. These two were perpetually hard—especially around each other. Didn't they know? Didn't they see the furtive glances passed from one man to another? Like notes between classes, those glances. *Do you like me? Check yes or no.*

"That's right." Lock stroked his cock, and it distracted her.

She couldn't help but stare at the proud length of him. Paper-thin skin rolled over his cock, back and forth, caressing the veined muscle underneath. The head curved, plump and glistening—good enough to eat. She could almost taste him on her tongue, both the salty flavor and the velvet-smooth texture. He knew exactly what she was thinking, judging by his smug expression. And from the way his grip tightened, knuckles turning white.

"Hold her legs." He didn't move his gaze from hers while he spoke to Krist. Maybe he couldn't. In those molten depths she found the doubt he had to hide. She picked up his fears like Easter eggs and collected them in her basket. And carefully broke each one open.

Krist obeyed Lock; of course he did. He hooked his arms underneath her knees, spreading her apart. Without her legs to support her, she slid down his chest, feeling the abrasion of chest hair on her back. Her whole front was exposed, from her flushed cheeks to the damp folds of her sex.

Lock gave himself a few more pulls, rough ones, before joining them. The wicked look in his eyes made her clench around nothing. His gaze focused in on that pink, swollen place. His nostrils flared. Then he dipped his head and licked. Her mind went blank at the first wet touch of his tongue. Any worry or embarrassment was far away, tiny specks on the shoreline. They couldn't touch her where she floated in bliss.

Each swipe of his tongue made her hips curl up. The helpless undulation of her body pushed against Krist, and he groaned. Again and again, Lock made them writhe. He held them both on the tip of his tongue, like puppets on a string.

With Lock as their master, where he was always content to be. *Safe,* she realized.

Pulling herself out of the drugging sensations, she reached for him. Her fingers tangled in his hair, and then she tugged— hard. His head came up at her command, and hazy eyes slowly focused on hers.

"Fuck me," she said hoarsely. Because she wanted to tighten around *something* and his fingers wouldn't do. Because even he couldn't hide in his pleasure.

He didn't have to obey her. *Put your hand over her mouth,* he could have said. Krist would have obeyed, and so would she. But he reached to the nightstand and grabbed a condom.

"Put it on me," he said, shoving the packet into her hand.

With trembling fingers she tore the package and fitted the latex to his cock. He stiffened at her first touch but stayed still as she rolled it on. Completely still, even though she sensed the electricity moving through him with every warm touch of her hand. A muscle jumped in his jaw. It was like watching someone bite through the pain. It was like hurting him.

His finger dipped into her wetness and curled up. Checking her. Testing her. The empty foil wrapper fell from her nerveless fingers. Then his cock was there, pushing inside. And God. This position made her feel so full. He couldn't really be larger now, but he was, he was. He filled her up and expanded outward, pressing against the walls of her sex.

He pulled out, just a small ways. She braced herself, but the first deep thrust made her gasp anyway. Krist gasped too, swearing. Cursing them. His cock flexed behind her. He wanted *inside* somewhere. Inside her or inside the grip of Lock's hand. Krist deserved that much, but all he had was the flat plane of her back. Every time Lock pushed inside her, she rocked back to meet him. He used her too, rocking her against him in rhythmic movements that matched his hips. They worked with the same beat, playing a song only they could hear.

Lock kissed her. She was taken aback by the forcefulness of it. Even when he fucked her, when he *spanked* her, he kissed her tenderly. Always. He teased her mouth open and invited her to respond. Not this time. Now he claimed her. He plunged his tongue inside, invading her mouth the same way his cock did. His tongue felt somehow rougher now and burning ten thousand degrees.

He pulled away—his kiss, his cock. And then in again, fucking her and kissing her in one long, sinuous motion. Krist was there, opening her wider, jacking off against her back. They moved together, a writhing sea of three bodies and one goal.

Lock's kisses were like waves on the shore, leaving only to return again. She couldn't breathe in the interim. Didn't know what to make of it. Rough, coarse kisses. *Like he might use with a man.* This time when he reached for her, she let her head fall on Krist's shoulder. Lock wouldn't have had to do anything. He could have kissed nothing. He could have *fucked* nothing if he really didn't want to, but he did. Deep inside, he did.

His expression must have warned Krist before his movements did. She felt the catch of breath from behind her. Lock leaned forward and took Krist's mouth. Rough and coarse. She tried to watch, but she couldn't. Couldn't move. Couldn't interfere. But she felt it anyway. It ran through her body like a tactile thing. Like getting fucked from one more, unseen angle, and she moaned, helpless and already sorry.

It didn't break them, though. Thank God, it didn't break them. Lock groaned too, right into Krist's mouth. And Krist was making small sounds, unformed words. Their movements sped up, frantic and jerky. They were going to come. She could feel Lock's cock thickening inside her. Krist's hands tightened on her legs.

She couldn't even breathe like this, pressed between their bodies. She gasped and tasted their arousal in the air, as if it flowed all around them in a psychedelic sexfest. A color burst of sensation, and she could do nothing but take it. And then pleasure gathered in her center and exploded. It radiated out to her limbs, blinding her and leaving her open.

Lock came next with a hard thrust and a grunt that vibrated from his chest to hers. A sudden warmth on her hip came last as Krist followed them into climax. He lifted her once, twice more, using her body to wring the last of his orgasm onto her skin.

HAILEY'S BODY WAS slick beneath him. He pulled out, pulled back. Krist still gripped her thighs so tightly she'd have finger-shaped bruises tomorrow. "Let her go."

Krist lifted his face from the crook of her neck, held Lock's gaze as he slid his hands from her knees to her ass. Slow. Hailey's legs dropped, and she slipped from the cradle of his arms. Boneless, she rolled off the bed and stumbled out of the room. A few seconds later the shower blasted. They'd have a few minutes without her pressed between them, pulling and pushing and urging. His pulse slowed as the endorphins leached out of his bloodstream. Crashing.

"Are you done?" The bed creaked as Krist rolled onto his side, his voice a raw whisper.

"You should go now, before she gets back." The longer he and Krist were apart, the more he wanted this interlude over, the harder it was to remember why it had felt so right between the three of them.

"You're a bottomless pit. I just keeping going down further, and further, thinking this will be the end. This is where it stops. But the more I have, the deeper I get, the more I want. Shit you'll never give me."

Lock knew that feeling, that terrible slide toward destruction. Seeing it reflected back at him made him feel hungover, like the bed was spinning and if he could just get his leg on solid ground, it might stop. "What do you want now?"

"Quit fucking with me and just fuck me already. Or leave me the fuck alone." Krist swung his legs over the side of the bed and grabbed for his pants, prickly hurt rolling off him in waves.

"Stop." Krist froze with his jeans bunched around his knees. Lock pushed down a knot of angry panic. "Did I tell you that you could leave?"

"Well, you didn't tell me to stay. And I'm not staying if you just want to use me to entertain your girlfriend."

Girlfriend stung. "I thought you liked being used."

Krist stood, zipping his pants. "As long as you keep doing it. Use me, fucking use me, but don't shove me in a drawer afterward like some forgotten dildo."

The shower stopped. His pulse stuttered; he needed to finish this before Hailey came back out. He couldn't let her smooth this over, scold them like unruly children unwilling to decide on a game to play. He chose the game. He made the rules.

One shove and Lock had Krist flat on his back, bed bouncing beneath them. He yanked the still-unbuttoned jeans down his legs and left them tangled around Krist's ankles. He watched as Krist's cock hardened. The weight of his regard, the anticipation of what would follow the shove, was enough to bring Krist right up to the edge.

Lock rolled him onto his belly and pinned him to the mattress with the length of his body. Wrapping his arms around broad shoulders, he wedged one arm between Krist's chest and the bed and squeezed. Holding him down. Holding him still. He pressed his face into the plane of Krist's shoulder and bit down hard. Anchored in the moment until he released. "I don't forget anything, but if I wanted to fuck you, I'd have done it already."

Lies. Growling them didn't make them true. The cruelty, salty like the skin he still tasted on his lips, felt right. Abrasive. Cleaning the wound. He couldn't give Krist what he wanted, only what they both needed. A sharp pain to remind them that nothing changed, nothing mattered. Full or empty. Drunk or sober. The hurt remained. If he fucked Krist, he'd be making a promise he couldn't keep.

Lock couldn't see Krist's face, but felt his whole body tense beneath him. "This was a mistake, and you can't even blame the booze."

CHAPTER FIFTEEN

Sunday morning

HAILEY WOKE UP surrounded by sex. It wasn't the musky scent of Lock's warm skin when she nuzzled close. It wasn't even her own flavor that he fed her from his fingers. This was something else, an undefinable energy in the room, the dregs of intimacy. Coffee would drown out the scent of them but not the awareness vibrating through every cell of her body. He burned against her back. The sheets felt like sandpaper against her skin. Cool air hardened her sore nipples. Like the minutes right after climax, when her clit ached at the slightest touch—only this was her whole body. Too sensitive. Too used to handle anything else, but the world didn't let up.

Krist's absence pulsed through the room, a gaping wound in a wild-beast night. She wouldn't think about that. She felt Lock's heart beat slow and steady through the arm slung over her body, and in his cock, hard and hot against the small of her back. *Don't think about that, either.*

The sleek alarm clock gleamed eight a.m. on the second day, and she hadn't yet fulfilled her task. The most important reason for coming. Her sister. Family. *Redemption.* Their fucked-up family life hadn't been her fault, except…was it? Had she done something to make Chloe rebellious and reckless? Had Hailey done something to make their mother leave?

She rummaged through her bag and found a new outfit. Somewhere during the potent sex-ridden hours, she'd lost her confidence. The swagger with which she'd worn those fishnets and platforms the first night was missing. The leather skirt fit her hips awkwardly, as if she was trying to look cool and failing. The bra pinched her, and the top was more see-through than she'd expected. She still wore a costume, but the disguise was growing thin.

The elevator dinged open, and she winced. When she didn't hear anything from the bedroom, she stepped inside and hit the button for the lobby.

She'd find the father of Chloe's baby and convince him to… A wry laugh huffed out of her. She hadn't been able to convince Krist to stay the night. Hadn't convinced Lock to talk about what he felt when they'd lain alone in the dark. So odds weren't high she'd be able to convince this man to take responsibility for his child either. Except she had to. Her little niece or nephew counted on her. Hailey knew about the hurt that never left, the doubt that infected every relationship she'd ever had. Chloe had compensated by becoming the friendly girl, so damn accommodating she'd ended up pregnant. Meanwhile Hailey might as well have entered a convent, she'd become so reclusive. The man she spoke to most was the pastor of her church, and even he had gently suggested she attend the spring social, keeping an eye out for the bachelors. Neither approach, her sister's nor her own, had filled their small apartment with much warmth.

The bar area was dark and empty. No chatting up the bartender for information today. She followed the smell of coffee to a dining area around the side, separate from the swanky lounge. A large placard read *Complimentary Breakfast*. This room seemed far more comfortable, almost too homelike for the frosty hotel. Fat rolling chairs with thick cushions scooted up to oak tables. Along one wall, a line of banquet tables held platters and gleaming serving trays. Only a handful of people were seated at the table. A couple of kids—or were they teenagers?—worked together on the waffle machine, laughing when it bubbled from the sides.

Yes, this was exactly what she needed. Light streaming in through the broad open windows. Breaking bread amid laughter and pleasantries. A full belly to start her search.

Her stomach growled as she piled her plate high with eggs and bacon and a cinnamon roll so hot the icing still rolled down the side. Coffee, tea. Fresh orange juice sounded even better. Something wholesome to nourish her. Something real.

The man sleeping upstairs is real.

Pushing the thought away, she found a table in the corner. This seat gave her a clear view of the city unimpeded by surrounding buildings. Endless rows of glass and metal cubes as far as the eye could see, bleeding into the orange morning light, shattering it.

She wasn't the only one enjoying the view. At the table beside her, a young man scribbled in a notebook. He looked at the horizon, expression intent, before looking down to write quickly. Like copying down notes from a chalkboard. It made her look more closely, searching for the words scrawled there, the answers, but all she saw were pretty colors and a new day. That was what made her different from her pastor, who could divine truths from the world around them. It made her different from Lock, who plucked notes from the air and wove them into a song. Seeing something beneath the surface, capturing it. That had never been her forte, but in that moment, with her eggs cooling on the plate and the light almost blinding, something stirred inside her.

"Excuse me," she said. The young man didn't look up, so she called again. "Excuse me. Do you come here every day?"

He blinked as if surprised anyone else was in the room. She recognized him then as the guy she'd spoken to backstage, Colt. She'd felt something then too. He knew something. He could help.

He shrugged. "I'm up earlier than most of the crew. And I like bacon."

"Did you ever see a girl with the band…?" No, she corrected herself. A woman. Chloe was a woman, now that she was pregnant, and if Hailey was honest, she'd been a woman for a long time. They had both grown up fast. "A young woman about my age? She's an early riser too. Blonde hair, a little taller than me."

"That's a lot of girls," he said, but his gaze flicked away.

She slid into the seat opposite him. "Her name is Chloe. She's my sister."

Wariness shone in his eyes. And concern. "She okay?"

Her heart panged. At least someone here had cared. Was Hailey looking at the father of her niece? Because God, he looked so young.

"She's okay," she said softly. "I just need to find out who she was friends with here. I need to speak with them. Can you help me?"

He swallowed and said nothing.

"You knew her," she prodded gently. "You were friends with her."

He shook his head. "Friends, yeah. As much as anyone is friends around here. But not like you're implying. We didn't fuck, if that's what you're asking."

Hailey raised an eyebrow.

"Okay, I mean, I wanted to. I told her that, but she said she already had a boyfriend. They always do, right?"

"Who was her boyfriend? Someone in the band? In the crew?"

"Nah, some guy back home. And she never talked about him except for that. That's why I figured she was just letting me down easy. But what do I know; maybe he's real."

The knot in her stomach grew tighter. Some guy back home? No, there was no boyfriend. Hailey would know. She *had* to know, or what kind of sister was she? But no guy had come around to pick her up, and Chloe always came home at night. So when had she even had time to see a guy? Hailey's heart swelled in her throat, because God, she had failed worse than she'd thought.

Maybe he's real.

"Thank you," she murmured and stood. She started to walk away when he called her back.

"Hey, you gonna eat that?" He nodded toward her plate the next table over.

Her stomach did a little flip-flop. Her hunger had evaporated under the blistering heat of abject guilt. "Go ahead."

"Thanks." He gave her a small smile. "That was how I first noticed her. She always used to pray before she ate. Quietly but you could see her lips moving. I asked her about it once. She said it reminded her of home."

LOCK FOUND HAILEY in the bedroom with her overnight bag and her purse slung over her shoulder. Leaving. That couldn't be right; he still had one more day. "Where do you think you're going?"

"Oh, I was just coming to talk to you. I have to go home. I should get on the road before it gets too late. I hate night driving." Her voice lilted, fast and forced cheerful, but he could hear sadness leaking in at the edges. It made his jaw tighten.

"I'm not done with you yet. I decide when you leave."

The sadness sharpened into anger. "If I want to go, I'll go. My keys are still in my purse. The door is right over there, and I haven't forgotten how to use it. I may have signed a contract, but I didn't sell you my soul."

She hoisted her bags higher on her shoulder. His fingers itched to grab them and fling them across the room.

"You committed to three days." He kept his tone steady. She wasn't wrong, but he wasn't ready for their interlude to end. There were too many things he still wanted to do with her, to her. Every time he touched her, he came up with half a dozen more. Not enough time.

"My sister needs me."

"She called?" He hadn't heard her phone ring, but she might have it silenced. If something were wrong, he'd have to let her go. He'd put her on a plane himself.

"No. But I'm worried about her."

"She hasn't been very worried about you. She's selfish. She doesn't deserve you." He didn't deserve her either, but he had her anyway. For now. For a little longer.

"That isn't how family works. She's my baby sister. I take care of her."

"Who takes care of you?"

She winced, and he knew the answer was no one. Nobody took care of his little church mouse. She gave and gave until there was nothing left for herself, and then she gave some more.

"That's what I thought. Put down your bags."

She let them slide down her arm and land at her feet with a jingly *thump*. "Are you going to tie me to the bed and force me to stay?"

Jesus. The things that came out of her mouth. "Would you like that?"

Her breath hitched, and she wrapped her fingers around her wrist, stroking absently exactly where he'd bind her. And not with the soft terry belt of a robe this time. No, he'd cuff her and lose the key. Or find some rope. The rough stuff they'd used to tie equipment to the top of the van back in the day, before they'd had roadies and buses. He'd keep her. The tightness in his belly, the pulsing in his cock, that was lust, not need. He didn't need her. He wanted her. And he could keep what he wanted.

She licked her lips and nodded. "Or you could just ask me to stay. *Please* really is a magic word."

"But you don't want me to ask, do you, Hailey? You want me to hurt you, to make you, to use you. That's why you haven't touched those keys jangling in the bottom of your purse, why you keep coming back for more. I don't have to tie you up; you're already bound to me. You're mine." *Because I do need you.* The thought bristled, but it wasn't wrong either. He'd lied to himself for a long time, but not anymore. He'd lied every time he told himself he could stop with the next drink. There hadn't been any stopping then. And there wouldn't be any stopping with Hailey. He took two long steps, closing the distance between them, and covered the hand stroking her wrist. Squeezed, just hard enough to still the subtle motions that were so like the ones she'd used the first time she'd touched his cock. She melted into him, her forehead falling against his shoulder, and murmured something into his chest. He couldn't hear her, only feel the brush of her mouth. Wet and hot, dragging a trail of syllables ever closer to his nipple. The tip of her tongue touching and darting, again and again. He skimmed a hand up her back, gathered her hair in his fist and guided her lower.

She dropped to her knees, and he flicked open the fly of his jeans. His heavy cock sprang free, slick with precum, and nudged her cheek. There was nothing tentative in her touch now. She looked up at him from beneath lashes heavy with unshed tears, smiled a wobbly smile, gripped the base and guided it home.

Was she saying good-bye?

Her free hand disappeared under her skirt and between her legs as her cheeks hollowed. He could feel her rocking against her fingers, a counterpoint to her swirling tongue. Even now, taking care of herself. He was a fucking monster. A selfish prick with a selfish prick. "Stop."

Her hand stilled, but she kept a steady pace on his cock, the muffled *mmph* of an apology vibrating up the length. That's not what he'd intended. He released her hair, pulled himself free from the warmth of her mouth with a groan. Brows knit with confusion, she wiped her chin. "Did I—What's wrong?"

"Nothing, baby." Everything. They might be bound together, but he couldn't keep taking from her. He'd use her up until nothing was left. Drink every drop until he was alone at the bottom of her bottle. Still—always—thirsty. He bent, gathered her into his arms, and guided her to the bed.

Standing before her, he drank her in with his eyes. He'd use his hands and his mouth soon enough. The scrap of leather skirt rucked up to her hips, exposing pale blue panties, so wet at the crotch they'd gone sheer. He nudged her knees apart for a better view. The blue suited her, not the skirt. Not the filmy top either. Not him.

He grabbed the hem of her shirt, and she lifted her arms so he could slip it over her head. The bra was wrong too. Cheap and shiny, the band digging into her chest. He wrapped his arms around her and flicked the clasp open. Her sigh of relief, a broken pant against his chest.

He pushed her onto her back and yanked her panties down her slim legs, savoring her surprised gasp. He left the skirt behind, something he could hold on to when he buried his face between her legs. Just one more taste. One last drink.

Kneeling, he bit the soft flesh of her thighs and soothed the marks he made with a roll of his tongue. Her every cry as he worked his way up, a reward and a reminder of what he was. He wanted to rub his cheek into the warmth radiating from her core. Instead he pursed his lips and blew a cool breath over her slit until she shivered. She tangled her fingers in his hair, petted and pushed.

"Yes, baby. Yes," he hissed, making her shiver again. "Take what you want. I'll take care of you."

He would take care of her. Like this. Only like this. He grabbed her right hand, the one she'd teased herself with while she blew him, and shoved her fingers into his mouth. Sucking hard, tasting and slicking. Then placed them between her legs. "Hold yourself open for me."

So pretty, her delicate fingers splitting pink folds. For a moment all he could do was look and inhale the salt of her skin.

"Please," she begged.

He broke all his toys. Ruined everything he touched before it could be taken away. And now he had Hailey spread open and twitching beneath him, all wide eyes and packed bags. Still unbroken, ready to stay if only he asked. He didn't want to break her anymore. He wanted to save her. *Please is a magic word.*

He didn't have any magic left in him. He'd washed it all

away in a shower of booze and debauchery. *Please fuck me. Please hurt me. Please love me.* Was that the fans echoing in his mind, or Hailey, or his own weak-willed soul rattling its cage? He could give them all most of what they wanted. Fucking and hurting. The kind of angry fucking he needed like water and air and whiskey. He stilled. He needed this, wanted it so badly his whole body ached, but it would only make the voices louder, the rattling worse.

GOD, HE WAS so gentle with her. Something had changed. She'd felt it happen with her mouth around his cock and her hands cradling his balls. Now he bent between her legs, all breath and shadows, heat and softness. It was like having her pussy licked by a stranger.

She wanted Lock back.

With a soft yank of his hair, she pulled him away. His eyes were unfocused, his expression unbearably soft. It was almost enough to make her put him back to work, to press his face down until she came, adding more wetness to the shine on his stubble.

But it wasn't really him. Not the man who had lured her up to his room that first night, the one who had demanded her signature on his sex contract. Ink on the page, straw spun into gold, a sex fairy tale come to life.

Flipping over, she knelt on her hands and knees—presenting herself to him. She could imagine the view: her ass displayed lewdly, the plump lips of her sex visible beneath. It was a rude position, almost cruel in its offering, but she had to make it worse.

She turned back to meet his dark gaze. "I need you."

For a long moment he simply looked at her. The thick bulge in his leather pants didn't let her feel too bad, but he still didn't touch her. Cool air made her shiver, writhing like bait on a hook. Her own desire was the hook, sharp and unyielding, holding her in place for him.

Slowly, so slowly he reached for her. A large hand down her thigh, stroking. Soothing. Measuring.

"What do you need from me, Hailey?"

He wanted her to say it. "I need you to...to fuck me."

"Is that so?" Two fingers slipped inside her, blunt and jarring and not nearly enough. He twisted his fingers, finding a place that shot sparks through her core.

"God."

"Like this?" His fingers moved in and out. He fucked her with his hand, and she thought she was going to die.

"Please."

"I'm waiting."

"Fuck me with your cock. Now. Hard."

He chuckled behind her. "That's a lot of instructions." His fingers were gone. Empty. Foil ripped; heartbeats passed. Then his cock pressed to her opening, slippery and smooth. "This is one." He pushed inside her, all the way, and she gasped in relief at the fullness. "And that's two. Now about that third one..."

She tensed in anticipation. *Hard.*

His hand tangled in her hair and pulled taut. Her hands clenched the sheets. He withdrew and then thrust back inside, sudden and rough. Exactly what she'd asked for. So much more than she'd expected. It hurt. Oh God, it hurt, the pressure so intense, the pleasure a form of pain. Her inner muscles spasmed around him, trying to keep him out, trying to pull him in. He ignored her silent pleas and thrust again—harder and harder, faster and deeper until she couldn't tell where she ended. It felt like her pussy had joined with him, merged in some kind of new being, one that could fuck all day and all night.

An eternity passed before he let go of her hair. Her head dropped onto the sheets. Her shoulders too. He kept going, unstoppable; she didn't want him to stop. He pushed her into the mattress with every hard thrust, pressing her, flattening her. She became liquid, an ocean stretching out, and he was gravity—down, down, down. She lay flush against the bed, barely able to breathe, immersed in his groans as they rippled around her.

He came with a sudden jerk of his body, his hands tightening on her hips, his teeth sinking into her shoulder, marking her. Wait. She ground her hips in a helpless rhythm, pushing back into his invasion, pressing down against the mattress, needy and hopeless. She couldn't join him. He rocked over her in tiny bursts, keeping his own pleasure going while she clenched around his cock even though it wouldn't be enough.

His hand slipped beneath her hips. The first touch of his fingers to her clit made her jump. He drew circles with her wetness, steady, focused despite his languor. She felt him soften inside her, and she squeezed until he grunted and pulled out.

A sigh escaped her, vague disappointment and sexual malaise. She wanted to come, but only at his hand. On his cock. Against his mouth. Her fingers had become a second-rate option. What would happen when she left? The knowing slide of his fingers swept those thoughts away. She humped his hand, mindlessly, artlessly, and even the pillow-top mattress became an instrument of pleasure. This bed, which had housed so many rock stars and millionaires, so much sex and discontent—and then there was her. She came in a small, tight climax, her plaintive cry soaked up by the springs beneath her.

They panted in the aftermath, his fingers still swirling in her sex, dipped into the mess left behind. Would his fingers be wrinkly from all that wetness? How long would she leave her mark?

"Stay," he murmured against her back.

The word was a request. It had to be. They both knew the contract couldn't hold her. It was a cage without a door, enclosed on every side except the one that mattered most. But his quiet voice chained her more than sheets of paper ever could. The weight of his body. The beat of his heart against her back. Stay.

Her voice was muffled against the bed. "My sister. She needs me."

"I need you."

Her heart clenched, surprised that he'd admit it. There was a distance when he spoke to her back, a confessional wall where he could whisper his wanting of her. But she wouldn't sit behind the veil, wouldn't let him give her false reverence. She was still wet from fucking him—still sore, for God's sake.

She turned over. Her gaze held his. "Not like that."

"Like what then? You can send her money." He added, "I have money."

Was he offering to pay her? "That wasn't part of the contract."

Fuck the contract. She expected him to say that. He wasn't a man who respected rules, even ones he'd set himself. But apparently this one mattered.

"We still have one more night," he said.

If he demanded they follow the letter of the contract, that meant she'd leave in one day. One day where Chloe wondered what the hell her sister was doing. One day while her little niece or nephew grew into the size of a kidney bean.

One day of being irresponsible and aimless. Of living only for herself.

Like he did.

She reached up and petted his hair, soothing the sting she'd made before. "I'll stay."

It felt like a reward when he kissed her, long and slow. But when he pulled back, his expression was almost mournful.

"What's wrong?" she asked.

He smoothed her hair and kissed her again. Distracting her. And God help her, she let him. His hands moved over her body, wakening her. Again?

Yes, again, his body answered.

He was ruthless in his pursuit of his pleasure. He made it an art form, this dissolute living. Almost stylized in its perfection. And so damned tempting she couldn't turn away. She wanted him to teach her his secrets, like a magician to his apprentice.

And above all, she wanted him to remember her when she was gone.

CHAPTER SIXTEEN

MOE RAKED HIS fingers through his wild hair and paced the length of his suite like a caged beast. He stopped beside the leather sofa, a smaller version of the one in Lock's room, and sat on the arm. "I don't like this. You flying ahead of us is not the plan."

Lock slouched deeper into the plush recliner. He made the plan. He could change it. He was only telling Moe as a courtesy. "You wanted an extra day to play tourist; you got it. I need out of this hotel, out of this city."

"You need a meeting." Moe sneered. He might as well have slapped Lock in the face. The truth always hurt, but Lock wouldn't give him the satisfaction.

"Screw that. I'm fine."

"Yeah, just like Krist."

"What's he got to do with anything?"

"Who do you think he came to after you booted him last night? Take care of your shit. I'm not cut out for being in charge."

Moe in charge? If Lock weren't so pissed, he'd laugh. "It's none of your business."

Moe launched himself off the couch and resumed his pacing. "No? Your dick nearly destroyed this band once. I think that makes it my business. I know I joke, but I will not be some

Behind the fucking *Music* punch line."

Always that. If his mother's past wasn't swinging around his neck like a goddamn albatross, it probably wouldn't have even mattered. But the media loved a scandal—and a family curse. "How long do I have to pay for that? It could've happened to any of us."

"But it didn't. It happened to you, because you were so far in the bottle you didn't even know what was happening half the time."

He could barely get the words out through his clenched teeth. "I'm not drinking."

"Fine. Then get your head out of your groupie's ass, sweet as it is, and apologize to Krist. Make this right. If we fuck up another tour, we can kiss the label good-bye."

We? How about him? Their agent's words rang in his head. *The label will replace you if they have to.* The guys didn't even realize. Everything they'd built, none of it really belonged to them. They'd sold their souls for a private jet and a six-album contract. They were all expendable. "I will. When we're all in Vegas."

"Now." Moe tossed something at him. A flash of orange. His lucky guitar pick. "Tell him to get up here."

Lock slipped his phone from his pocket and swiped his thumb over the screen. *Come to Moe's room.* He flicked his pick over his knuckles the whole time he waited.

Moe let Krist in, and they both settled on opposite ends of the couch. He'd come, Lock half expected him not to, but Krist wouldn't look him in the eye.

"The last time we all sat around a hotel coffee table, it was your intervention," Krist said.

Moe laughed, thumping his fist against his knee. "Burn!"

Lock gnawed the inside of his cheek. Yes, because his sobriety, or lack thereof, was such a joke. "I thought you didn't want to be a punch line."

"Sorry, man. But that was a good one."

Krist covered his mouth, hiding a smirk. Assholes, both of them.

"Fuck this. I'm leaving tonight. I don't even know why I bothered to tell you."

"I think you have some business to attend to first." Moe jerked his head in Krist's direction.

Right. He'd accepted the pick. The bargain was made. "It's between me and Krist. Get the fuck out."

"It's my room."

"Moe, please?" Krist kept his gaze on his lap as he asked.

"Okay." Moe stood, pointing at the both of them. "But nobody fucks in my bed but me."

Lock felt all the air sucked out of the room with the slamming door. He didn't have anything to apologize for; he hadn't made Krist any promises. Hadn't done anything Krist didn't want him to do. The only difference was Hailey. She'd seen something in him, brought something out of him that hadn't been there before. A kindness. A yearning. And Krist had gotten caught in their undertow. That part wasn't fair.

"I'm sorry, Krist. I know what happened was too much."

"Whatever. It's cool." Krist pulled at the loose threads surrounding a hole in his jeans.

"I can see that it isn't."

"Am I hurt? Yes. But it's on me. You don't have that much power, Lock. No matter what you think."

"I don't think—"

"Shut up. I appreciate the apology, even if it was under duress. Just don't lie to me."

He could do that at least. Tell the truth. "Okay."

"Why are you heading to Vegas early? To get away from me?"

"No." The lie felt too easy; he backtracked. "Yes."

"You know Moe thinks you're drinking again. I thought so too until last night. Now I just think you're going to self-destruct all on your own. Go to Las Vegas. Run away. Do whatever it is you think you need to do. Just don't take the band down with you."

"I won't."

"I can forgive you for a lot of shit, but I won't forgive you for that."

HAILEY SHUT THE flat plastic cover on the window, blocking out the orange sunset. Would it get brighter when they were in the sky? Hopefully Lock liked the dark. She stared straight ahead at the faux wood paneling. Or maybe it was real wood. Private jets probably had the best of everything, down to the plush leather seats. Her fingers gripped the arms, drawing crescents with her nails.

Footsteps warned her of Lock's approach, and she shut her eyes. If he thought she was asleep, he wouldn't talk to her. He wouldn't ask questions.

"You all right, babe?"

Or maybe he would. She nodded but didn't trust herself to form words. At least, words other than *help* and *oh God* and *I'm scared*. The plane pulled forward in a series of turns that made her insides twist.

He settled into the chair beside her, rustling the leather and sending a wave of his subtle musk to calm her. "Because you look like you might puke."

"I'm not going to puke." Mostly because there was nothing in her stomach. She hadn't been able to eat the preflight supper at the small airport. Lobster with cream sauce and asparagus with goat cheese. Even thinking about it made her stomach turn over.

"Okay," he said in a contemplative tone. His fingers were warm and dry against her palm. She startled and pulled away, but he caught her hand. "Relax. We'll be in the air soon."

That's what she was afraid of.

"I'm fine. Really." Her words were somewhat betrayed by the high pitch of her voice. God, why couldn't she be smooth and classy and blasé like a hundred other women could be—and had been? Why did she have to be so…like herself?

He would see right through the clothes and the sway of her hips and the wild sex she'd never really had before. He'd see how boring she was, and if there was one thing she had learned about the rock-and-roll lifestyle in the past two days, it was that boring was a cardinal sin.

"You ever flown before, Hailey?"

Oh, the way he said her name made her feel strangely alert. A fraction more in tune with him than the airplane surrounding them. He had that kind of voice: magnetic, melodic. Thousands of people packed into a stadium just to hear him, and she couldn't resist him either.

The plane picked up speed. His thumb made circles on her palm, around and around, giving her courage.

She took a deep breath. "There weren't a lot of family trips, if you know what I mean."

He didn't pause, not even for a moment, just one circle around the other, one breath and then another. "I don't really know what you mean, but I hope you'll tell me someday."

Someday. Oh God, she wanted someday. But they only had

one day left. She wasn't sure she'd be ready to bare her soul—or her family's sordid past—by tomorrow. But for the first time, the thought of not opening up, of not being vulnerable, terrified her. Like watching the threads break one by one and knowing she would fall.

She liked the circles he made, but she wanted more. She wanted him to sing to her. But she couldn't ask him to do that. It seemed like too much, even if he had done it for thousands of people last night. He wasn't a puppet who had to perform when she pulled the strings.

A sudden image came to her, of Lock's agent berating him for something after the show. And then again on the way to the airport. Schedules to keep. Commitments to make. So maybe he was a puppet after all, but she wasn't his master.

"Will you...will you talk to me?" she asked, suddenly desperate to hear him.

"About what?"

"Anything." They were down to hours, and she needed every pitch he could make, every breath and groan charted in her mind, a map to study in later years. *I went there once.* A story she would tell herself.

He was quiet a moment. "There were a lot of family trips for me, if you know what I mean. But they weren't really vacations. They were business as usual."

She looked at him then. The overhead panel bathed his face in a soft light, as if he glowed from within. He'd lost the edge she'd seen before, almost as if the ritzy hotel had made him sharp. Hackles. Defenses. But they were down now.

"What was the business?" she asked.

"Music, of course. You didn't know? Cate James. She was famous back in the seventies for breaking up Royal Velvet. But then she hooked up with my dad and the rest..." He made a sweeping gesture toward himself, the plane. Everything.

"Is history," she finished softly.

"Yeah, I got pretty comfortable on planes. Didn't always end up on the same flight as my parents. There were scheduling conflicts. Tutors for me and rehearsals for them. And break-ups. My parents were always on the verge of divorce. Sometimes they'd split for a few days, sometimes for months. That's how I met Krist. My mom hooked up with his dad while they were touring together. It didn't last. Nothing lasted. Except the party, but I wasn't supposed to know about any of it. Just read about it in the tabloids like everyone else."

Her heart clenched. She imagined a little boy reading tawdry headlines and trying to understand. "That must have been tough."

He chuckled. "Poor little rich boy. Don't waste your worry on me, beautiful."

She shook her head. He wouldn't want her sympathy. But she had to know… "Why did you follow their footsteps?"

"Everyone I knew was in the business. I guess when other kids want to get away from their parents, they go to college. I went on tour."

"Just like that?"

"Put the band together. Worked our asses off. Just like that."

"I didn't mean to imply—"

"I know you didn't. Lifetime of inadequacy at work here. I don't want the special treatment or the expectations that come with being Cate James's son, but I get it anyway."

She knew all about that, how she could never escape her mother's shadow, how she would forever be deemed unworthy. "I'm sorry," she said, though the words were inadequate.

Their gazes met and held, a conduit for silent messages.

His: *My path was set a long time ago.* And hers: *Mine too.*

He looked past her to the window, which was still closed. "Don't look now, but we might be ten thousand feet off the ground."

"What?" She slid the covering up, and sure enough, they had somehow lifted off without her even noticing. Her brain had ignored everything but his words, that voice of his like a furnace, melting everything in its sphere.

She touched her finger to the glass, surprised to find it cool. Outside, the orange glow had mellowed into something gold and glowing. The clouds formed a puffy blanket beneath them.

"My God," she breathed. "It's beautiful. Majestic. Do you see it?"

He had a strange expression on his face, watching her.

She blushed, embarrassed. "But you've seen this so many times. It's probably boring."

When he spoke, his voice sounded different. Almost strangled. His hand tightened on hers. "No. Not boring at all."

LOCK DREW HAILEY'S hand to his mouth and brushed his lips over her knuckles. Alone in the cabin with her, watching the sunset and holding hands. It was like they'd taken a rocket to the moon instead of a hop from Midway to McCarran.

He couldn't remember the last time he'd just held hands with a woman. Maybe he never had. The kind of life he led wasn't conducive to shared quiet moments. Alone or in a crowd, no middle ground. It's probably why he'd brought Krist in, to battle back the overwhelming quiet building between him and Hailey. Only it hadn't worked. It bound them together more tightly, let her in deeper and pushed Krist further away.

The tightness in his chest had nothing to do with the changing cabin pressure. One day. They had one day left together, and then his life would return to normal. What would she go back to? A troubled sister. A job she loved. Some guy from around the corner who'd spring for movies on Friday nights, fuck her gently, and take her for granted.

That last part burned the most. He tapped the CALL button on the console above their heads.

The flight attendant appeared seconds later. Brisk and efficient with his starched uniform shirt stretched across narrow shoulders, he held his hands behind his back. "Yes, sir."

"Bring a bottle of sparkling cider and strawberries if we have them." He remembered the bliss on Hailey's face that first morning when he'd fed her pancakes and berries while she sat naked beside him. Simple pleasures. He could give her—give himself—more of those.

"Right away, sir."

Hailey squeezed his hand. "Are you celebrating something?"

He was. Every moment they had left. He'd celebrate them until she couldn't stand to leave. "You."

"No champagne?" Her brow knit with confusion, and was that hurt? Oh God, she still didn't understand. He wasn't asking for fucking cider because he didn't think she was worth champagne.

"Hailey, I've been sober for a little over a year. The go to detox after you've basically ruined your life and the lives of everyone around you kind of sober. We're not having champagne because there isn't an ounce of booze on this plane. I'm not having champagne because..." The word's caught in his throat, but he had to say them. She needed to know. "I'm a recovering alcoholic."

She paused. "That's... That's wonderful."

"It's what?" Instead of recoiling from his weakness, her face broke into a smile that rivaled the sunset out the window. She leaned across the armrest and planted the softest kiss on his lips. A sweet balm to the raw exposure aching under his skin.

"Really. I'm so proud of you. A year is fantastic. We'll celebrate that too."

He shouldn't have expected anything less from Hailey, from his girl. *His girl.* She wouldn't turn her head and gawk at him like he was an accident on the side of the road. No, she'd just beam at him like he'd done something amazing.

Because he had. His sobriety was a fucking miracle.

The attendant parked a cart beside their seats, uncorked the bottle with a pop, and filled two glasses. Lock half expected him to click his heels. "Will there be anything else, sir?"

He released Hailey's hand so he could take the useless glasses. He wanted to drink from the hollows of her collar bones, sip from the tips of her breasts, lap from the folds of her sex. "No, and unless we're crashing, you stay in the back. Got it?"

"Of course, sir. I'll be back to collect the cart when we're preparing to land."

Lock didn't want to celebrate anymore. He wanted to revel.

CHAPTER SEVENTEEN

THE RICH SCENT of freshly brewed coffee filled the fellowship hall. Usually Tim would settle at a table near the back with a steaming cup and a pile of Mrs. Markum's chocolate trifle. Last month he'd done exactly that, only Chloe had sat with him, teasing him about the predictability of his potluck dessert choices.

There's got to be twenty different sweets up there, and you settle for pudding? she'd said.

It's not just pudding. Look. There's brownies, candy-bar bits, whipped cream—

Don't forget the cherry.

The way she'd said *cherry* was a sin. All round and full, with a cocked eyebrow and wet lips. Purposeful. He could only nod and take the bite he'd dangled on his spoon.

Tonight Chloe avoided him completely. That she'd shown up at all surprised him. At first he thought maybe she'd changed her mind about his proposal. But anytime he approached, she suddenly had very important things to do on the other side of the room.

Was it really so wrong, wanting to take care of her? He couldn't help that.

So he stood there at the end of the buffet, coffee and trifle in hand, unsure of his next move and only half aware of the murmur working its way through the crowd.

Pastor John hurried toward him, expression grim. *Did he know?* Tim's cup rattled in the saucer.

"We've got a situation. Some of the older kids are sharing a video, an inappropriate video—"

Relief coursed through him. It wasn't about him. That happened with the kids from time to time. He'd find them huddled in a corner, giggling, and counsel them about modesty and purity of thought. Hypocrite that he was. "I'll go."

"No, you don't understand. Tim, it's…" He rested his hand on Tim's shoulder and lowered his voice. "It's a video of Hailey."

It didn't make sense. How did the kids have an inappropriate video of Hailey? How did an inappropriate video of Hailey even exist? Maybe there was some other Hailey he didn't know. "Hailey *Miller*? Chloe's sister?"

"She's on the news. A few parents have already cornered me. They want her fired."

"Fired? We don't even know anything yet. Are we even sure it's her?" Tim's heart raced. Chloe would be devastated. As much as she talked about wanting to take care of herself, it was Hailey who did the caretaking. What would happen to them? His gaze flicked to her. She stood by the giant punch carafe, surrounded by church ladies with apologetic looks on their faces. And smirks. They were telling her. Delighting in it. *Not very Christian of them.*

"I only saw part of it, but even with the censor bar—It's her and it's bad."

He wanted to abandon Pastor John and go to Chloe, put himself between her and whatever was happening, like a human shield. So he did. He crossed the room, catching stray comments as they rose over the din. Brightly lit screens dotted the room. Ugly punctuation points in a hateful conversation.

"Well, you remember their mother."

"Disgusting."

"Not watching *my* kid."

"We knew the sister was bad."

Did they hear themselves?

Anger welled in his chest. Hot molasses. An alien sensation. Someone stopped him. He should know this person, but his mind was so clouded the face didn't even register. And when this person spoke, it was like pots and pans clanging in Tim's head. "Will you be taking over the nursery until they find a replacement?"

Taking over? Replacement? They'd tried and convicted her in minutes, and he hadn't even seen the evidence yet. Didn't need to see it. All he needed was Chloe.

"No, I will not." His voice came out louder than he'd intended. A boom that hushed the crowd. Folding chairs scraped linoleum as people turned to see what new scandal would entertain them tonight. His stomach rolled. They'd convict him too if they knew Chloe was carrying his child. Too young. Out of wedlock. *Narrow-minded...* "If you fire Hailey, you can fire me too. Have you all forgotten about glass houses and stones?"

Pastor John shook his head. "Tim, this isn't the time. We'll discuss it later."

"There is no later. Are you going to let this continue? Are you going to fire her? Abandon her?"

"She's found a new income source." A voice from the crowd. It matched the *disgusting*.

Pastor John frowned. Resigned.

Tim was resigned too. Literally. "I quit."

The collective gasp sucked all the air out of the room. Let them suffocate on their righteous indignation.

CHLOE STARED AT Tim from across the sea of parishioners. He stared right back.

Protests sprang up—first one, then another. Bursts of color in a harsh wasteland. "But you didn't do anything wrong."

"We don't want *you* to leave."

They were talking to Tim, of course. Tim, who had graduated with honors with a masters of divinity. Tim, who welcomed every lock-in, potluck and choir practice. Tim, who had gotten sucked into the Miller sisters' vortex. It wasn't his fault. No one would blame him.

First Chloe had seduced him. She couldn't even pretend it had been otherwise. She was everything they would accuse her of, when her tummy grew large and obvious.

And now Hailey...*what had Hailey done?* Chloe didn't even know. Mrs. Wilson had said something about a video. About a musician? It was hard to tell, but it was bad. Even Pastor John looked grave, and he had always been welcoming to them, even knowing who their mother had been.

Her stomach lurched, and she clapped a hand over her mouth. Oh God. Oh no. *Not here.*

But then Tim was at her side, his arms around her, guiding her. The crowd parted for him—of course it did—and she closed her eyes against the faces. Macabre expressions of horror and prurient interest. She felt the weight of that scarlet letter suddenly stitched onto her T-shirt, except instead of *A* for adulterer, it would be *S* for seductress or *J* for Jezebel. She was a full alphabet of condemnation, and she wasn't even sorry.

None of these people had ever cared about Chloe—or even Hailey, who had been so nice to everyone, always. Who had taken the best care of their kids. Let them rot in hell for all she cared.

All except Tim. He loved this place. *And now he was going to lose his job.*

"Where are you taking me?" Her fingers muffled her words.

"Bathroom," he murmured. Tim pushed them into the main hallway. They weren't alone, though. She could feel the eyes on her, laserbeam judgment, cutting her open.

"No. Outside." She needed to get out of here. She needed to *breathe* again.

They made it into the courtyard near the back, adjacent to the playground, and at least here it was empty. Pine needles formed a crunchy carpet on the loose cobblestone. She broke away from Tim's hold and leaned against a thick tree, panting.

"Are you going to...?" His voice was cautious.

She laughed roughly. "Throw up on the statue of Mary? Don't worry. I get crazy nauseous, but nothing ever comes out."

"Let me help you," he said in a low tone that tugged at her. Earnest, that was him. Earnest enough to give up his career— his *community*—to stand up for her. Or her sister.

She pulled out her phone and googled the name of the band. First three hits were YouTube videos. And there was Hailey. A very naked Hailey on her knees. Oh Jesus. Had Hailey seen this? It might not be her. *Please let it not be her.* But if it wasn't, it was a damn good look-alike.

And Hailey had been MIA over the past forty-eight hours.

More than enough time to sneak backstage and end up banging the guitarist. Chloe should know. She'd worked that gig—well, she'd worked the merch counter. But she'd also flirted with musicians and roadies and everyone else who wasn't Tim.

"Fuck." The word bounced around the empty courtyard. At least the video didn't seem to have sound attached. Not that it mattered much.

Tim touched two fingers to her arm, and she looked at him. His expression was sad—so sad. Had she done that? Was all his grief now for Hailey and none for the marriage they wouldn't have?

"I'm sorry," he said, and it hurt that he meant it.

"Hailey will land on her feet," she said, not quite believing it. The old Hailey, she could handle anything. This new Hailey, who went on weekend benders to bang rock stars? Chloe wasn't sure she even knew her.

But she wanted to.

"You don't have to quit your job for her," she said. "It probably won't even change their minds. We'll find something else."

His eyes darkened. "You think I did that for her?"

Her stomach flipped again, threatening revolt. She pressed a hand to her stomach—still flat. How long until it grew? How long until that flip turned into the kick of a little foot?

"Who did you do it for?" she whispered.

The baby, she thought he'd say.

He shook his head. "This is my church too. Or it was. We don't shun our friends, our neighbors, without even talking to them."

"And if she did do this? If this is her?" And it was. The timing was too perfect. Or imperfect.

"We don't evict people for a single mistake." He shut his eyes, looking pained.

She was *hurting* him, but she couldn't stop. "What if it wasn't a mistake?" she whispered. "What if she *liked* being with that guy? What if she's not sorry for her sins?" They weren't even talking about Hailey anymore. She knew it, and so did he.

His jaw clenched. "Is that what you think I want from you, Chloe? An *apology?*"

She stepped closer and put a hand to his chest. Like she'd done yesterday, although she wouldn't be falling to her knees this time. Wouldn't unbuckle him in the open courtyard. There were limits—even to her own depravity.

They were a breath apart. She could feel him waiting with each warm not-kiss against her lips.

"Prove it's not," she whispered, and she didn't mean sex this time. Lust wouldn't be enough—not for a lifetime. Not for marriage.

"What do you want me to say? I gave up my job for you. I *proposed* to you."

Tears threatened, but she wouldn't back down. Not this close. "I love you," she whispered.

He sucked in a breath. "Chloe…"

That was more than a flip in her stomach. It was like getting punched there. "We can be friends. We don't have to—God, you don't have to be a fucking martyr for me."

"No. We're not going to be *friends.*" He sounded furious. "Why does it matter so much? Why do you have to hear the words?"

Because I deserve it. She didn't say that though. Didn't want to hear his denial—that no, she didn't deserve a husband who loved her. That was for other girls, with other mothers, ones who weren't the church's pariah. She clenched her jaw and let his words wash over her.

His gaze softened, but the words still stung, like seawater—finding every raw spot in her past. "You just take and take, and there's not going to be anything left of me. What am I going to have left?"

And then she couldn't hold back anymore. The fear of being pregnant, the humiliation in the rec room—they rolled down her cheeks in hot tracks. "Me," she said simply, hopelessly, already knowing it wouldn't be enough. She was never enough.

Something broke in him then. She watched it happen: the tiny fissure turning into a crack. A fissure that let her see his horror at her words, his shame. His love. Why did she have to hear the words? She didn't—not if she could look at him deep inside, without that guarded restraint. It kept him back from more than a blowjob. It kept him back from *this*.

"You're afraid," she said finally.

"I'm not." His voice sounded thick. Like she did before she broke down and cried—no, after. "I'm *terrified*. All these years, it's just been me. Just me. No one counts on me or expects anything."

Did he really not see? "Everyone counts on you, Tim."

He shook his head. "It's not the same. I can unlock the door and pour pretzels into a bowl. It doesn't matter what time I come home."

"I'm not going to stick a tracking device on you."

"No, I *want* you to care. But the thing is, if I marry you, if I *love* you, I'd care too. And you're…too much for me. You're so full of life, and I've ruined it now. You should be out following the band or doing whatever you want to do. And now you can't, all because I couldn't keep it in my goddamn pants."

"Tim." She waited until he really focused on her. Damn, those deep, soulful eyes. She hadn't stood a chance, really. Even though it was kind of insulting that he'd thought she was her mother, she couldn't blame him. She'd thought so too. "*Tim*. I'm not going to leave you."

He looked stricken. "I couldn't take it if you did."

She tackled him then. It felt like the right thing to do, and it felt even more right with his unsteady heart thumps by her ear and his arms around her waist, pulling her tight.

"I'm not leaving," she said fiercely.

He pressed her close until her nose was smashed into his shirt and his fingers were cutting off the circulation in her arms—still not close enough. It would have to do. His breath huffed warm against the crown of her head. "I love you," he murmured.

She sighed, feeling it slide home. "I know."

CHAPTER EIGHTEEN

HAILEY JOLTED AWAKE as the plane bumped against the ground a second time. The plane was small enough that she could feel the spring in the wheels, bouncing thousands of pounds of metal into the air before settling on the runway. The sudden lurch jerked her forward. Only the seat belt kept her from falling.

"Lock?" she mumbled before she had her bearings.

He didn't answer. His head was resting on her shoulder, his body slouched enough to make up the disparity in their heights. She gently nudged him back so that his head was cradled in the plush headrest. His mouth hung open, so unguarded in that moment, almost…innocent?

Where had that thought come from? He was the wolf, and she was the girl with the picnic basket, the fishnet stockings cloaking her as much as a red riding hood. But when he snored softly and clenched his fists where they hung off the armrests, she couldn't deny he looked painfully vulnerable.

He *was* vulnerable. He'd admitted that much to her. A recovering alcoholic. She knew exactly how brutal addiction could be. She'd watched it destroy her mother. It scared her a little, as if he might go on a bender and slap her face like Mom had done. But Lock was sober now.

And she wouldn't be around long enough to help him stay

that way.

The plane pulled to a stop, and she nudged him. "Lock?" she whispered.

He grumbled something unintelligible.

Her lips quirked, and she brushed dark hair from his forehead. It was softer now, lighter without whatever styling products he normally used. She ran her fingers over his scalp, relishing the small moment of intimacy, a glimpse of quiet power before he woke up and snatched it back.

Sounds came from the front of the plane. Probably the stewardess or captain preparing for them to depart. Curious, she pushed at the plastic covering on the window. Just an inch and the orange glow almost blinded her.

"Ouch." She slammed it shut.

A touch on her arm made her jump. She glanced back to see Lock watching her through slumberous eyes. Oh yes, there was her wolf. Her grabbed her chin and tugged her close, capturing her lips in a languid kiss. He fucked her with his tongue, hard and possessive, stealing her air and her peace of mind.

A throat cleared.

Hailey jumped back, startled and embarrassed, but Lock held on tighter. His hand cupped her neck, holding her still as he finished with slow licks of his tongue against hers.

When he sat back, his expression was smug. Or maybe it only seemed that way to her because of how much he'd enjoyed himself. His lingering satisfaction hung in the air like incense, smoky and sharp. Even the flight attendant who'd interrupted them seemed to sense it.

He cleared his throat. "Sir, ma'am, I—"

"We'll come out when we're ready," Lock said lazily.

"Yes, but—"

"You're dismissed."

He looked dismayed as he ducked back through the curtain.

"Mean," Hailey chided.

Lock's shoulder raised in a half shrug. "Maybe he'll learn not to interrupt."

Wry amusement made her smile. "Do you assume everyone is here to please you?"

His gaze darkened, sweeping down her body and back up again. "Twenty-four hours, sweetheart. And I expect to be well pleased."

Heat spread all the way to the tips of her ears, and he chuckled.

"Let's go," he said. When she reached for the bags, he shook his head. "They'll follow with our stuff. It's just you, me, and a fifteen-minute ride in the stretch limo to the hotel."

She flushed again, though this time it was more arousal than embarrassment.

The captain waited at the door. He opened his mouth to speak—to thank Lock for his patronage? They were all fawning around him, every doorman and driver and waiter. All adoration, reverse patrons who were paid by his art.

Lock brushed by him, holding on to her hand so that she was forced to wave a hasty *thank you* and *good-bye*. She turned back to the plane to do so, and when she faced the front, the brilliant sunset hit her like a tactile force. Only Lock's grip on her—tightening, too tight—kept her moving forward.

She heard them first. Shouts and mechanical whirs. She felt them second, bodies pressing around her, grabbing her, so many.

Was it a publicity stunt?

What does Moe think of the tape?

Did you know you were on camera?

She saw them last, a thick swarm of people surrounding the plane like goddamn locusts. They held notepads and cameras. A flash went off, and she was blinded all over again.

Something tripped her, and she stumbled. Would have fallen but Lock hauled her up again. He dragged her through the crowd, his fist around hers like a vise, barely glancing back, never speaking a single word—not to her, not to the press. He was impenetrable, like a warrior moving through an enemy army, and she was just the limp and battle-scarred flag trailing behind him.

A hand yanked the clip out of her hair, and something else tugged on her shirt. There were too many of them, all around; she couldn't breathe. It felt like drowning, in flashing lights and endless questions instead of water, while the grasping eddies ripped her to shreds.

Suddenly she was free. Walls of black closed in on her, but that was okay. At least she could breathe in this man-made shelter.

Bodyguards, she realized. Security had arrived, not quite in time. They formed a fortress around her and Lock, moving them quicker than before. Their hands grabbed her too—not to take from her, but to push her forward and into the car.

Falling, stumbling, she landed on butter-soft leather seats. Lock was on the opposite side, panting.

She managed to push herself to sitting. "What…the hell…was that?"

"Fuck if I know."

The limo pulled out quickly, fishtailing before straightening out. Lock got on the phone with someone—his agent?—and corresponded in a series of grunts. "Send it to me," he said before ending the call. Then he watched something on his phone while she watched him.

"What is it?" she whispered. It wouldn't be good. That much was clear.

When Lock's eyes met hers, he smiled. Though that wasn't the right word for it. He grimaced, maybe. But even that was too tame, too complacent to describe the expression he made.

He bared his teeth. Like a wolf. Only not the sensual animal she had learned to love. This was something far more dangerous, a feral creature who would ruin her without remorse.

"Do you know what those vultures were doing there?" he asked, deceptively calm.

"They were taking pictures of you."

The smile again. Not a smile. "And you, sweetheart. They were taking pictures of you too. You're famous."

"FAMOUS?" HER MOUTH hung open in shock.

As soon as he'd seen the crowd on the tarmac, he'd known there was a problem. The swarm of paparazzi, like wasps to a target, was more urgent than any he'd seen in a long time. His first thought had been that something had happened to one of his bandmates. Krist dumping his motorcycle on the interstate. Moe decking an asshole in a bar fight. Then he'd heard the questions.

Did you know you were on camera?

Déjà fucking vu.

Was there more than what he'd just watched? What else was waiting to slither out of the darkness and bite him on the ass? He eyed the phone Hailey had clutched in her hand more than half the time he'd known her. Did it take video? Of course it did; all of them did. And she'd been poking around the hotel, looking for her sister's baby daddy. Like that was a real plan.

She'd just stumble over the roadie her sister had fucked. Where? Waiting in line at the ice machine or having a drink in the lobby? He was an idiot. She could've passed some cash to a security staffer, leaked that elevator footage herself.

If this spiraled out of control, his days with the band were done. The only real family he'd ever had. And Krist would never forgive him.

"Give me your phone." Anger and betrayal simmered just under the surface of his careful calm. Soon it would slip, and he couldn't stop it.

"Excuse me?"

"Give me. Your fucking. Phone."

Her hand shook as she extended her arm in compliance. She didn't even have a lock screen. He skimmed her contacts and checked her photos. Nothing recent. Nothing to indicate she'd been documenting their time together. He landed on a selfie of Hailey with a younger woman who looked vaguely familiar. The sister. He wouldn't peg them as sisters separately, but cheek to cheek he could see the similarities in their smiles and the shape of their eyes. The love between them radiated; they glowed with it. Better than any stupid Instagram filter. It pissed him off. It pissed him off more that he didn't find anything. No lurid video. No night-vision app.

Before he could return the phone, a message popped onto the screen.

OMG! Are you on TV?!? Call me. Now.

"And your sister knows. She seems excited." He tossed the phone back to her.

"Knows what? What's going on, Lock?" Hailey fumbled the slick plastic and found the message. "Why am I on TV?"

So innocent. A wolf in a sheepskin cardigan, skipping to the slaughter.

He reloaded the video his agent had forwarded—Hailey and Krist on their knees in the elevator—and turned the screen toward her. "Because you look like an angel and suck dick like a pro."

"Oh no. Oh God." She pressed her fingers to her mouth. Tears trailed down her cheeks. Was she that good an actress?

"Tears won't help."

She sucked in a sharp breath and wiped beneath her eyes with the heels of her palms. "No, I guess they won't. Nothing will. Not if that's on TV."

"Oh, they won't play that on TV. Well, maybe on cable. Last time I had a sex-tape leak, they used stills with censor bars and put the video on their websites behind adult-content warnings."

"I'll lose my job. I'll lose everything." She paled. Her voice, barely above a whisper, quivered.

It hit him then. *She wasn't acting.*

This wasn't something she'd done to him. He'd done it to her. Put her in this position. Cost her. *Everything.*

"Shit. We can't go to the hotel. They'll be camped outside every possible entrance." He thumped on the glass behind him, and the driver slid it open. "Are we being followed?"

"Not that I can tell, sir."

"Good. Stay alert and find us a dive motel." No room service. No leather couches. No luxurious linens. Just a bed and a chair and a quiet place to hide Hailey until he figured something else out. "We can't put the genie back in the bottle, but I can do some damage control."

SHE STUMBLED INTO the dark motel room, bumping into Lock. At one time it would have been sexy to feel him, large and warm in front of her. It would have been comforting.

But that was an illusion.

Lock found the remote and filled the room with a yellow glow. There they were on the evening news. How was this news, anyway? *Because he's a rock star, idiot.*

The blurring tools barely covered anything. Her lips were visible around some blurry gray pixels. The side of her breast was there, the dark pixelated nipple looking pretty damn similar to her real nipple.

Lock's phone rang, and he swore. "This is my lawyer. I've got to take this."

She nodded numbly, but he'd already turned away.

It didn't matter. Years of playing the good girl, and she'd managed to fuck it all up in forty-eight hours. A lifetime of trying to *not* be her mother, and she'd managed to become the scorn of the entire country. Forget that small-town stuff, with the dark looks and whispers. She'd hit the big time with her promiscuity—wouldn't Ma be proud.

Clapping a hand over her mouth, she only just made it to the bathroom before retching. The toilet in this random motel was only marginally clean, but she hugged it like it was a life raft in a storm.

Lock's low voice came from the motel room. He sounded pissed. "Find out who the fuck leaked the video. Fire them. Sue them. Make it fucking rain."

That made her feel better. Like one percent better compared to ninety-nine percentage points of total suck.

The crazy thing was how he'd demanded to see her phone. *And your sister knows. She seems excited.* Did he think Chloe had something to do with this? Like some sort of groupie thing?

But she couldn't imagine anyone wanting to be exposed like that, fan girl or not. Her stomach twisted again, but when she leaned over the bowl, nothing came out.

With a groan she pushed herself up. There wasn't any toothpaste or a brush, but her mouth felt too disgusting to wait. She unwrapped the little bar of hand soap and licked it before rinsing with the provided Dixie cup. She was washing her own mouth out with soap, but it couldn't clean her, not really. The dirtiness went skin-deep, all the way inside her to the desires she'd never told anyone before. No, she'd kept all those secret wishes to herself, until Lock came along, her personal sex genie.

She stared at herself in the mirror. Dark circles were under her eyes, standing out like bruises. When had that happened, in the last ten minutes? Or earlier, in the sex-crazed two days with Lock? Which one of those things was making her look so defeated?

Maybe both.

Clean. She needed to get clean. She turned on the shower. Cold spray rained down on her outstretched hand. No matter which way she turned the knob, the water stayed chilly. That didn't matter either. She stepped inside and pressed her face right under the nozzle, letting it fill her eyes and her nose, so she didn't have to cry or breathe or hurt.

How much time passed? She was shivering.

The shower curtain was yanked back with a startling screech of rusted metal rings. Lock stood there, looking furious. "What the fuck are you doing?"

"Showering," she said, though the word didn't come out clear, not with her teeth chattering.

He narrowed his eyes, incredulous. "You have your clothes on."

She glanced down. Her black T-shirt and miniskirt were

drenched. Her toes sloshed when she wiggled them in the three-inch heeled boots. "Oh."

A beat passed as she swayed on her feet. Would he leave her now? She imagined him walking out of the motel room, getting into his limo, and leaving her here. *Of course he should do that. You're having a mental breakdown.*

His expression was…stricken. "God, baby. Come here."

"No, I'll get you wet." But her words came out muffled against his chest. He pulled her out of the shower and flush against his body. Warm. *So warm.* It almost hurt where his body touched hers, but she couldn't push him away. She couldn't make her arms and legs move at all, so he had to undress her all on his own, as if she were a doll.

He pulled back the thin bedcovers and tucked her in. She was cold again, inside the scratchy sheets with the vent blowing on her. She wanted Lock's furry legs to slide between hers. She wanted his chest against her back.

"Lie with me?" she asked.

The regret on his face answered first. "I have to figure this out. And besides, you need to sleep."

Sex. He thought she was offering him sex. Well, why wouldn't he think that? She'd done it again and again.

His expression softened, turned faintly pleading. "Just rest, okay? It will seem better when you wake up."

It would seem better, maybe, but it wouldn't *be* better. He was right when he said they couldn't put the genie back in the bottle. There was no way to take back all the videos currently streaming on TVs and YouTube channels. There was no way to unsign the contract.

There was no way to stop falling for a man she'd have to give up by tomorrow.

CHAPTER NINETEEN

Monday morning

IT WAS DAY when she woke up. Only a sliver of light shone, beaming bright between two heavy drapes, but it was enough to drag her from heavy sleep.

Her head spun. Blindly she groped around for the warm limbs that would be tangled with hers, but the sheets were cool to the touch. *Lock.* How had she gotten hooked on him so fast? He was like the drugs her mom didn't do and the men she didn't sleep with outside their marriages. He was a poison that seeped into her bloodstream and made her want more.

The clock read eight a.m. She'd slept through the night, all without him touching her. He'd whispered a million dirty things last night and delivered none of them. He'd told her it would seem better in the morning, but it didn't. Broken promises.

So much for getting things in writing.

A dark form lay on the other double-size bed. He was on top of the covers. She crept closer—quiet, quiet. One arm was slung over his head. His mouth wasn't open like it usually was during sleep. Now he looked tense, angry, teeth clenched against some unseen hurts.

It made her want to climb in beside him. She wanted to be the big spoon and cuddle away his pain, exactly like he hadn't done for her last night. He'd slept on the opposite bed, and even though she knew it was probably kindness, or even chivalry, that hurt even worse. She was no longer the sexy groupie he wanted to exploit. She was the innocent girl again, the one he needed to protect.

Stretching raised a hundred sore spots on her skin. Bruises and abrasions. As if she'd been in the fight of her life instead of just a sex-crazed couple of days.

Her bag and purse were neatly stacked near the door, along with some black luggage that must belong to Lock. She found her toiletries and clothes and made herself presentable in the bathroom, trying not to glance at the toilet so her stomach wouldn't turn over.

God.

A blinking light caught her eye from the floor, underneath the sink. Her phone. It must have landed there when she was busy puking her guts out, but before the awkward clothed shower.

Ten messages, all from Chloe.

Seriously, where are you? Are you okay?

You looked great, if it's any consolation. Really hot.

That was probably the wrong thing to say. Forgive me?? This is crazy.

A pang of guilt hit her, because she should have definitely called her sister by now. Hailey would have been freaking the hell out if this had happened to Chloe, so the least she could do was *call*. Still, she didn't press the button to dial. It still felt too…raw. A knife pressed into the flesh of her throat, teetering on the edge of her windpipe. If she moved fast or in the wrong direction, it would be over.

Hailey scrolled down to the last message from her sister. It read: *Please let me know you're okay. I'm scared.*

And then she had no choice. She had to call then, because she'd sworn never to let her sister be alone and afraid. Their mother might have left and Hailey might have thrown up every night the first two weeks in grief and fear, but it didn't have to be like that for Chloe. That was a promise, the kind she would keep regardless of any sex contracts.

The phone rang, tinny from the small speaker, echoing off the dingy tile walls.

"Hailey?" Chloe's voice was panicked, and another wave of remorse hit Hailey, threatening to send her doubled over to the toilet again.

Her voice was still hoarse from last night's episode when she spoke. "I'm fine, Sis. I'm sorry I didn't call sooner."

"Tell me where you are right now. Wherever it is, I'll come to you."

"No, you can't…you can't fly like that."

"Yes, I can. I'll drive. Or I'll ride a dragon. I don't even care. Just let me come get you."

Tears sprang to her eyes. God, when she had nothing else, she had her sister. It was a gift she hadn't even acknowledged. Hadn't even *wanted* to acknowledge. As long as she was the big sister, the caretaker, then she'd never had to worry about being abandoned. But they were both adults now—even Chloe's nineteen counted as such—and either one of them could leave. Either one of them could walk out the door, leaving only a disconnected number to be reached at. Either one of them could end up like their mother…and they each had been like her, in their own way, but they were still their own women. They could still choose to come back.

That firmed her resolve. "I don't need you to come get me.

I'd feel better knowing you're safe anyway. Don't worry about me. I'll figure it out."

Starting by going home. She ended the call and ignored the little twinge that said home was no longer a six–hundred-square-foot apartment in the middle of nowhere. The man sleeping on the bed—still tense, still somber—wasn't home. He was a wrong turn. He would take her for a ride and then spit her back out again, worse for the wear.

In the bottom of her bag was a rumpled copy of the contract, signed by both her and him. She snagged a pen from the nightstand and circled the subsection marked *Confidentiality*.

*In the event that the contents of this contract or its resultant acts
are made public, this contract may be terminated immediately.*

That was for his benefit, but she used it for herself. She draped the VIP lanyard Lock had given her over the folded pages. Had it really only been two days ago? It felt like a lifetime, as if she'd always been the girl sitting in the wings flashing rock stars, a backstage pass nestled in her cleavage. But the truth was, she was not that girl. She never would be that girl again. It had been a whirlwind vacation and identity crisis all rolled into one—and it was over now. She walked out the door of the motel without even looking back. And kept on walking, down the sidewalk until she found a cab.

Hailey was going home.

Lock would never really hurt her, not with his fists or even cruel words. But he'd hurt her anyway, just by not trusting her, when he made her sign the contract. And their time together hadn't changed that, because he still hadn't trusted her when the video broke—which was why he'd checked her phone.

He hurt her just by being *him:* a sex god, a famous musician, a man of excess and depravity. Someone she could never have a future with. That part hurt worst of all.

HE WOKE ANGRY and disoriented, slick with cold sweat. Another dark hotel room, lit only by the glow of a muted television. Another time zone. His nostrils flared against the scent of stale cigarette smoke, and he bolted upright. *Who booked us this shit hole?* As soon as his feet hit the scratchy carpet, he remembered. The flight and the video and devastated Hailey.

He'd spent the night trying to soothe her. When he'd run out of platitudes, he'd murmured song lyrics, nonsense, anything to keep her from panicking more. When she'd finally fallen asleep, he'd called everyone. He wanted a plan, but no one answered except Moe, who told him to clean up his fucking mess.

He could take his lumps, but Hailey shouldn't have to take them too. They could deny it was her. They could trot out a decoy, some starlet who wanted the attention. He'd seen it done. If his agent would just answer his messages. The clock on the nightstand flashed nine o'clock. So, eight in Chicago and six in LA. The phone would start ringing soon. Keep her out of the public eye for a few more hours, that's all he had to do.

Bang. Bang. Bang. The whole wall rattled with every thump on the door. "Room service."

The fuck? He peered through the peep hole to see the oversized forehead of the sleazy desk clerk from last night. A crumpled paper bag clutched in his hands.

"Go away," Lock said.

"Hey, Mr. Big Shot. I'm just trying to help you out. I could go back to my desk and start tweeting about asshole customers."

He knew that jerk had figured out something was up last night. Throwing extra cash at him to avoid using a credit card had been a mistake. It wasn't like his stage name was on his cards. But he definitely hadn't wanted Hailey's name tied up in all this. *Stupid.* And now this weasel was going to black mail him.

He cautiously opened the door and growled. "What do you want?"

"Thought you might be used to better accommodations. A few creature comforts." He thrust the bag at Lock. He hesitated to open the surprisingly heavy bag, not wanting to find a horrible surprise inside. Used condoms. Worn panties. Fans could get weird.

"Just some breakfast sandwiches and a little hair of the dog."

Shit.

Slowly, like something might pop out and bite him, he opened the offering. There, nestled in with hash browns and sausage biscuits, was a bottle of Jim Beam. He pulled it out, watching the amber liquid slosh. The asshole knew what he drank. Used to drink. "I didn't ask for this."

"My privilege." The dude wiped his nose on the sleeve of his filthy flannel and held out his hand. For a tip.

"Hang on." Lock tossed the bag in the trash and set the bottle on the dresser so he could fish out his wallet. He plucked two crisp fifties from the billfold and dropped them into the grubby outstretched palm. It was easier than arguing. He couldn't afford a scene.

"Pleasure doing business with you." Lock watched him slink down the hallway and closed the door.

"Hailey? Babe?" He called into the silence. No answer from

the bathroom.

The room was too quiet, the rattle and hum of the air conditioner the only sound. A hacking cough pierced the stillness, someone choking to life in an adjacent room. If he could hear that, he'd hear Hailey padding around. He unmuted the television and let the drone fill up the empty space in his head. Maybe she'd gone looking for food. Not a bad idea, he surely wasn't going eat the paper bag brunch from hell, but she should have woken him. What if someone recognized her? He paced in the small space between the two beds, step, step, turn. They'd be screwed. Did she have a room key? Money? Any idea where they were at all?

And then he heard his name. Not from Hailey's lips, from the overly glossed mouth on the screen to his right.

The Elevator Tape *isn't as polished as Lock's previous work. We don't know if they're going up, but bassist Krist Mellas and that mystery girl are sure going down.*

This was bad. They'd identified Krist, his damn tats giving him away. And soon they'd have Hailey's name. Fuck. He grabbed his shirt, yanked it over his head, and checked the clock again. Only five minutes had passed. Folded white pages caught his attention, pinned to the dresser with that fucking bottle of Jim Beam. When his hand made contact with the neck, his skin crawled. It shouldn't. It hadn't before. He should be able to touch a bottle to move it out of his way without it affecting him. Was it even the bottle? Or was it the papers underneath? Because he knew what they were before he picked them up. *The contract.* Blue ink circled a particular passage. *Terminated.*

She wasn't off to find breakfast. She was gone.

He'd failed on every level. His vision blurred. A tightness seized in his chest. And he was so thirsty. So thirsty he could drain the Great Lakes and still feel dry. Raw. Thirsty like sandpaper lined his throat and only a burning flood could clear it.

No. He was angry and weak, but he would not do this thing. He could touch a stupid glass bottle and not open it. Not drink it. He reached for it again, and his hand trembled. He pounded his fist into the dresser top to make the trembling stop. The cheap laminate cracked, reverb vibrating up his arm. It felt good, this pain he could tie to a specific action, this destruction he'd wrought on purpose. A power chord.

He kicked the bed he'd slept in alone. The skanky bedspread pissed him off. He'd lain on that all night. He'd tucked Hailey underneath one just like it. He'd checked them into this nasty pit because he'd failed. Because he was fucking weak. Because he couldn't keep his hands to himself and his dick in his pants. Because he was a piece-of-shit alcoholic addict who destroyed everything he touched.

He deserved this room. He deserved worse.

And then he was slamming everything. Punching and clawing. Kicking and stomping. His body wild and beyond reason. Nothing was safe. Not the remote or the lamp or the stupid drinking glasses with their sanitary wrap. Not the painting of a buck bolted to the wall. Not the darkness. He yanked the dank curtains from their track and lost his balance, falling to the floor in a tangled heap, surrounded by musty fabric and debris, releasing a cloud of dust and filling the room with light.

Oh God. He'd done this. Destroyed a hotel room like a rock-and-roll cliché. If only Colt could see him now, that would be the end of his hero worship. Nobody knew how hard he worked just to maintain some semblance of normal, how often he failed. The kid was better off without the spotlight, the celebrity, the fucking pressure. He shook, the adrenaline leaching out of his bloodstream, leaving him cold. The loss of control was as frightening as a blackout drunk.

He yanked himself free, sweat and grime a sticky film on his clammy skin, and stood to survey the wreckage. The bottle, unbroken, spun on its side in the corner of the room. Four steps and he was on it. The glass was smooth and cool in his hand. One long step and he was in the bathroom. He broke the seal and poured it down the drain. Steady.

He hadn't failed Hailey. He'd failed himself, by thinking he still couldn't face his own demons. He stared himself down in the mirror, the scent of the whiskey turning his stomach. He had and he could.

His phone beeped. He had to dig through a pile of torn pillows to find it. One missed call from Krist. The only call he wanted, other than Hailey's. God, did she even have his number? No, she didn't.

"I fucked up, bro." In so many ways, in all the ways—

"Are you still sober?"

—except for the way that counted most. "Yeah."

Krist's sigh of relief crackled their connection. "Then we can fix this."

"How? They've got your name attached to this thing too. Soon they'll have Hailey's. They'll eat her alive. It's snowballing. I don't know what to do. You said you wouldn't forgive me for destroying the band…" He dropped to the pile of bedding on the floor, the weight of this conversation too much to bear standing.

"This won't destroy us if we don't let it. And you're not worried about the band right now, are you?"

He was, but it was second on the list. His biggest concern,

his first and last thought, was Hailey.

"I can't let her deal with this alone."

"Do you love her?"

The question brought him up short. "What does that have to do with anything?"

"Relax. I'm not on your jock or anything. I have an idea for how to fix this, but it fucking sucks for me. I am not making the call unless you love this girl. Unless you want to ride off into the bullshit happily ever after sunset with her."

Is that what he wanted? A sunset ride into always? After three days? That was insanity. Except…her absence pained him. He knew he didn't want to wake up in another hotel room without her, and he'd never felt that way about anyone before. "Yeah, I do."

Krist sighed again. "I thought as much. You know Madeline Fox?"

"The pop diva? From the kids' show?"

"Diva is right, but she's done with the kid stuff. I think she might be able to help."

"What? How do *you* know her?" It didn't make sense. Krist didn't party with pop stars.

"Ward hooked us up for a musical play date. Doesn't matter. What does matter is that she knows a thing or two about making a spectacle. And I think she'll do me a favor."

"What kind of favor?"

"One that'll get people talking about something other than your dick. That girl can't sneeze without someone drafting a press release."

"Okay."

"Give me an hour. I don't know if it'll help or not. You owe me either way."

CHAPTER TWENTY

HAILEY TRUDGED INTO her apartment, bracing herself for her sister's anger. Well-deserved anger, because Hailey had gone off the rails. It was like she'd funneled every selfish impulse from the past few years into a single weekend. When she'd stayed up late to help with Chloe's drama project or when she'd woken up early to do laundry so they'd both have something to wear, she'd *thought* that was who she was. A good sister. A good person.

Poof. She'd signed that stupid contract and turned from Glinda the Good Witch into the Wicked Witch of the West. Disappearing from her life, abandoning her sister. She'd even called in a fake sick day just to hit the full three days of contracted sexual bliss. Well, she was a little sick—if temporary insanity counted as sickness.

That was all over now. And next on the agenda? Sleep.

"Chloe?" she called.

No answer. She could feel the stillness in the apartment too. It was empty. Of all times, she could hardly blame her sister for not letting her know where she was. A slightly hysterical laugh bubbled out of her. She'd lost any right to demand explanations ever again, but maybe that was for the best. Her sister was an adult now. It was time Hailey started treating her that way.

She took a hot shower, enjoying the massaging spray of hot

water on her aching muscles. The flight plan had included a six-hour layover in Madison, which meant she arrived home late at night despite her early start. It also meant her back had bunched into knots from hours curled up on two plastic airport seats, watching the still frames of her naked body on TV.

Cringing, she remembered the press speculation when she'd boarded the plan.

The fact that this mystery woman hasn't come forward indicates she wasn't doing this for attention. If she were a paid escort, exposure could mean criminal prosecution in the state of Illinois.

Paid escort? They meant prostitute. Somehow she was more offended on behalf of Lock and Krist. As if a woman would have sex with them for attention or for money… instead of the real reason. They were incredibly sexy, virile men, and any woman should be so lucky as to kneel beside them.

Although she had a hard time feeling lucky right now.

When she got off the plane, things had been impossibly worse.

Sunday School Teacher or Sex Worker?

They'd figured out who she was. How much worse could this get? She imagined press trucks parked outside the church, blocking all the parking spaces. She imagined the curious stares of the parishioners. Part of her wanted to stick her head in the sand, but morbid curiosity got the better of her. After dressing in loose sweats—a far cry from fishnets and high heels—she flipped the TV on, expecting to see herself invading the local news. Instead there was someone else's mostly naked body twisting and writhing on the screen. Dancing.

Pop star Madeline Fox was arrested late last night, but that's not the surprising news. The surprising part was who did the arrest-

ing—namely, the Secret Service, after the performer started a flash mob, complete with a mobile sound system and backup dancers, on the steps of the Washington Monument.

Well, that was the end of Hailey's fifteen minutes of dubious fame—and she was damn glad about that. Even if it was at the expense of this other girl. At least Madeline Fox might be able to sell some records out of it.

Tomorrow she might very well get fired from her job.

It was a good job. She loved the kids. And most important, the job had been the only thing available for an eighteen-year-old with no work experience or special skill set. Hailey had desperately needed a dependable job in order to keep custody of her teenaged kid sister. Well, Hailey had been taking care of Chloe for a long time, since well before her mother left for good, so at least she knew how to deal with kids. Pastor John had been kind enough to give her the job, but it was never supposed to be her entire life.

So maybe this was a blessing in disguise as well. If she got fired, she could take a chance on something she really loved to do. Which was…

Have sex with tattooed rock stars?

Hah. So maybe she didn't know what she wanted for a career. Figuring that out would be part of the plan. Besides, she didn't want to have sex with *other* tattooed rock stars. Just one.

Nope, wasn't happening. *Stop thinking about him.*

She searched the apartment for some clue as to Chloe's whereabouts. Her sister's room was surprisingly tidy. The haphazard posters and tickets and photographs stuck to the wall made it seem perpetually off-kilter, but there were no clothes on the floor or in the bathroom.

She would have worried her sister had also pulled a disappearing act, except there was a coffee mug in the sink. No, two coffee mugs. Her eyebrows shot up. Not that she could judge her sister, not that she *would* judge her sister, but damn. Chloe had never brought a guy home. Neither had Hailey. Their apartment had been inviolate from the less fair sex.

Until now.

Rummaging through her bag, she found her cell and texted her sister. *I'm home. Where are you?*

A minute later a call came in. "What do you mean, you're home?"

Even hearing her sister's voice sent relief through her. "Home. The resting place. The soft spot. You must remember it."

"The news reports said you were in Vegas."

"I'm old news. They stopped paying attention."

"It would have been nice if I'd known that *before* I flew to Vegas."

Oh shit. "No. You didn't."

But of course she had. Chloe was her sister. She'd known Hailey was in an emotional crisis, and she'd come to be with her. It was sweet but also…terrifying. "Where are you? At a hotel?"

"Nah, they wouldn't let us in. Didn't even tell us you'd checked out or what."

Suspicion rose up, along with a healthy fear of her baby sis alone in a big, mean city. "Who's *we?*"

"Me and Tim."

Tim from church. Trustworthy Tim who she could count on to look after Chloe. Oh…*oh.*

"Is he…? Oh God, he is, isn't he?"

"The father of the baby?" Chloe asked. "Pretty much, yes."

"I can't believe you let me think it was some roadie from

the tour."

"So you could march up to him and demand he step up before I'd even had a chance to tell him? No thanks."

"I wouldn't have… Okay, that's exactly what I did. Just to the wrong guy."

"Because you love me, Sis. I get that. But you have to let me work this out. I'm going to be a mother. And more than that…"

"What do you mean, more?" Hailey's stricken brain conjured images of twins and triplets.

"Oh, Sis. Don't be mad." Chloe sounded on the verge of tears.

That image morphed into worse things: Chloe hurt, Chloe scared. *The baby.* "What's wrong?"

"Nothing's wrong." Chloe sniffed. "Except that you weren't there. That's the only bad part. Everything else is good, Hailey. *So* good. I'm married."

Her mind went blank. "Married…to who?"

"Tim," she said, as if it were obvious. And maybe it should have been. But Hailey still hadn't quite wrapped her brain around the idea of Tim—trustworthy Tim—knocking up her little sister. That he would marry her after doing so should have been a foregone conclusion, but all she could think was *what if.*

What if Chloe had made a mistake? What if they couldn't trust Tim after all? What if something went wrong and her sister ended up hurt or afraid or *alone?*

Her chest panged, the same way it had when Chloe had first told her about being pregnant. Or maybe a little less painful. Maybe she was getting used to the idea of her sister as a grown woman. An adult. Someone who didn't need a big sister to hover over her anymore.

"I'm so happy for you," she managed to say despite the

cracking-open sensation in her ribs.

"Oh, thank God," Chloe gushed. "I wanted you to be there, but we were there at your hotel. Tim was demanding they tell us where you were, and they kicked us out. And the chapel was *right there,* right outside. It was a sign."

Hailey managed a watery smile. She made it through the rest of the conversation like the supportive big sister she had finally figured out how to be. The one who believed in her sister's judgment and would stand by her no matter what. Which left Hailey exactly where?

Alone in a small apartment, that was where.

All alone.

THE LIGHT WAS on in Pastor John's office when Hailey got to the church. Her stomach clenched in anticipation of what he'd say. She couldn't really imagine him browsing RedTube for sex-tape videos, but someone would have showed him. The thought of him disappointed in her—or worse, scornful—made her eyes sting with unshed tears.

But in a way, she was glad to see him. Even though she'd come during off hours, like a thief, sneaking around to steal her own belongings so she wouldn't have to see anyone, she was glad she'd have to face him. He deserved that much from her. He'd been so kind to both her and Chloe, and this was how she'd repaid him.

Public humiliation. The name of the church had even appeared in some of the articles.

Let's get this over with.

He always left the door open, with a welcoming policy to match. His head was bent, reading a book split open on his desk. Hailey rapped on the door frame to get his attention. When he looked up his expression morphed into one of…concern.

"Hailey. Come in. How are you?"

He didn't *seem* angry at her. Still, she knew he had to be. She was angry at herself. Her steps into the office were soft, careful, as if walking through a land mine. Sitting in the worn, comfy chair threw her into the past, when she'd sat down for a job interview—nervous and expecting the worst.

How was she? She was…torn. "I'm so sorry, Pastor John. Truly. I never thought that would happen; otherwise I wouldn't have—" She clamped her lips together, having no idea how to finish the sentence. Wouldn't have signed the contract. Wouldn't have had a threesome in an elevator.

And she wasn't even sure it was true. She might have done it anyway, because God…*God*.

She wanted Lock.

The pastor smiled slightly. "You've had a lot of support at this church since it happened. Several parents have spoken to me on your behalf."

A little shot of relief poured through her. At least someone had wanted her here. "Really? But I'm sure there were more parents who wanted me fired."

"Oh yes. Fired and brimstone," he joked, and she managed not to snort. Pastor John was always making puns. It reassured her that he could make them now, when it looked like the world had ended. As if things weren't as bad as they'd seemed on that long trip home.

He turned serious. "The parents aren't the only person. Tim stepped up right in the middle of potluck. Said he'd quit if you were fired."

Oh no. Her chest constricted. "You didn't do it, right? You told him not to?"

"I was going to speak to him, but he…well, to be honest, he disappeared." He gave a wry smile. "I've been fielding a lot of phone calls since then, but I have every intention of speaking with him. In fact, the board had just approved the job offer for him to become a pastor here."

Well, that settled it. She knew what she had to do. "In that case you definitely can't fire me. I quit."

His bushy eyebrows rose. "To make sure he keeps his job?"

"That's more important," she said.

Because he has a baby on the way. Because he's married to my sister.

She wasn't sure he had told Pastor John, though, so she didn't say anything. Besides, that wasn't the only reason why. Being a pastor was his dream. She hadn't even been that close of a friend to Tim, but she still knew that. And he was great at it. He was destined for the job.

While she…was destined to pine after the guy she'd left in a musky motel room outside of Vegas.

He looked solemn. "I know how hard you've worked, both here and with your sister. You deserve to have a long weekend off and not to suffer any consequences from that. But the preschool…"

"Is too important to risk," she said firmly. "Some of those families *need* this child care for their jobs, especially as afford-able as it is. And even at the low cost, the school is a profit center for the church. Don't worry about me. Seriously."

"I do worry about you," he said slowly. "And not just be-cause of this. I worry about whether you're comfortable here. It's hard to tell with you. You don't complain much."

He said it like it was a bad thing. She recoiled, feeling that familiar sting of not belonging.

"I tried my best," she said softly.

"Oh no, you were great with the children. We won't be able to find someone as good as you. That's a given. I meant you never seemed totally happy here. Not like Chloe."

She narrowed her eyes. Had he somehow gotten the sisters mixed up? Chloe was the wild, flighty one. Hailey was the staid, responsible one. "What are you talking about?"

"Chloe has always been enthusiastic about the church. She's full of enthusiasm and always suggests ways to improve things." He shook his head ruefully. "Sometimes we struggle to keep up with her, but she's exactly what this church needs. And I think this church has something she needs too."

She thought back, trying to remember whether it had been Chloe or herself who had gotten involved in the church. Hailey had gotten the job here, but it was Chloe who joined the youth group. Chloe who woke up every Sunday morning and banged around in the kitchen until Hailey dragged herself out of bed.

Chloe would make a wonderful pastor's wife. Unconventional, yes. But forthright and passionate and so damn caring. She loved this place.

Pastor John stood. "If you'd like to continue on with the church, I'm sure we can find a position for you in the administrative side."

She rose and helped him to the door. His arthritis acted up the closer they got to winter. "I appreciate the offer, but I think I'll use this time to figure out what I want to do."

He squeezed her hand before pushing through the door. "You'll come back and see us, won't you?"

She grinned, thinking she was about to marry into the family, so to speak. "I'm sure I will."

Then he was gone, leaving her alone in the church, standing

in the open-air foyer, usually sunbright, but now shadowed and silent. His car backed out, swinging headlights through the stained glass windows before pulling into the street. Hailey would pack up her few belongings and maybe the artwork her kids had made for her. Then she would leave this place and try to figure out what to do next.

CHAPTER TWENTY-ONE

THE WAITING WAS the worst. His whole body was wound up wanting to do something, but he couldn't do anything without a plan. When Krist's text message confirming that it was done finally popped up, he nearly jolted out of his skin. The relief spread through him like pins and needles, like a limb waking up after a long sleep. He hadn't destroyed their friendship. He hadn't broken up the band.

He read the "Breaking News" blog post, with accompanying cell phone pics, three times before it fully sank in. Madeline Fox had pulled some publicity stunt in DC. Chum in the shark tank. The media would swarm.

The grainy security footage of some no-name girl from nowhere would be all but forgotten.

Nobody had chased him down at McCarran. No cameras flashed at Midway. His story was already dropped. What was one more rock-star indiscretion compared to a teen idol spiraling out of control? Her handlers were probably going bat shit. He could sympathize. His agent, the label rep, his bandmates, they'd all taken their turn squawking in his ear. He didn't care. He only cared that Krist had come through for him. It was a gift—a parting gift from the brother he'd never had. A second chance.

Gotta find Hailey.

It wasn't hard. One Internet search, one flight, one very angry video conference with his lawyer and the manager of the hotel, and one rental car. He white-knuckled the steering wheel as he gunned it down I-90. There were only a few hours left before he needed to head back to Las Vegas, ready to perform. He didn't want to do it without Hailey sitting in the wings, preferably half-naked and with eyes only for him.

A slimy TMZ clone site had published the name of her employer under the headline *Sunday School Teacher or Sex Worker?* At least it wasn't headline news. His heart still ached. She wasn't a sex worker, and she was so much more than some absurd gossip feature about a Sunday school teacher he'd fucked on tour. She was his.

He let GPS guide him to the church listed in the article. It was a place to start. Someone there would know her and maybe even tell him where to find her. He tugged at the cuff of his button-down shirt. Probably not. Only the hardest of hard-core fans would recognize him dressed like this—fully covered and with a ball cap tugged low over his brow—but he was still a stranger. She'd just been splashed all over the news, and here was some random guy looking for her. Shedding the rock-and-roll trappings was surprisingly easy. He felt lighter, and not just because leather and chains weighed a ton. He would ask someone nicely. He'd even say *please*. He would find her.

He'd left *Lock* in the bottom of his suitcase. Keaton Shaw was driving now.

The parking lot was empty but for an ancient dented Toyota. Hailey's car. He remembered her describing it to the concierge he'd had fetch her bag that first night. A rusted-out beacon of hope.

He didn't need a sign, but it didn't hurt. He wondered what she was doing in there. Confessing her sins? Wishing she'd never met him? Praying he'd come after her? He crossed his fingers it was the last one and headed for the ornate doors.

Locked. Of course. He thumped his fist against the carved wood.

The door cracked open, and there she was. His little church mouse, tucked into jeans and a cashmere sweater that hugged her breasts. Her hair pulled back into a sleek ponytail. No more fishnets or glitter. No bed head. So beautiful stripped of her costume, even with her face all puffy from tears.

Her eyes widened in recognition. "What are you doing here?"

He tugged the brim of his cap. "Same as you."

"Collecting your things when you know no one will be around to see you?"

"Something like that." He touched her cheek, and she tilted into his palm just for a second before she recovered herself and pulled away. That hurt; he wanted her to lean into him. He wanted to hold her, to ease the worry knitting her brow. How could he do those things if she pulled away?

"I've never been fired before. I don't know how to *be* fired. They won't even let me say good-bye to the kids. What do I do when I run into them in the grocery store or the mall? Do I pretend I don't know them? I just—I can't…"

"Oh, baby. Let's get off these steps."

She led him through the vestibule into the church proper. Dark and cold and full of dust. Couldn't they afford heat? The urge to hold her close tipped over the edge of want and into need. It overwhelmed him.

"I missed you. I don't like missing you." He skimmed down her arms—his calluses snagging the soft cashmere—and pinned her hands to the top of a pew. Pressed his chest to her back. So warm. He'd write them a song full of warm forbidden places.

He'd write it now, on her skin, with his mouth. He kissed the back of her neck.

"Not here," she whispered in protest, but her body relaxed at his touch.

"Why not? We're alone. They can't fire you twice."

"I have to live in this community. It's still my home."

"It doesn't have to be." He nudged her legs apart with his knee, and she didn't resist.

"Are you going to whisk me away like some perverted fairy-tale prince? I think I read that story. It didn't end well."

"I can." He let her go, let the weight of their desire keep her still, and slipped his hand between her thighs. If she were wearing a skirt, he'd have his fingers inside her already. She should only wear skirts. He cursed the denim keeping him from his goal and cupped her, pressed against the seam of her jeans in time with the steady pulse beating between his own legs. "And it'll end so well you'll beg me to tell it again and again."

"What happens when you get bored with me?"

"I already told you, Hailey. You are not boring." He pawed at her fly until the button popped. Until he could tease the skin below her navel, right at the edge of her panties. "Tell me you believe me."

"I…" She arched back when he worked his way beneath the waistband. He didn't plunge inside yet, just held her, letting the warmth heat his palm.

"Try harder, baby. Think of all the ways you're not boring. The way you take risks. The way you know exactly what a person needs. The sexy way you move when I touch you right here." He split her folds, barely brushing the bud of her clit.

"Unh, I believe you."

"Good girl."

"But—"

He stroked her, jeans bunching at his knuckles, zipper scratching the back of his hand. "No buts. You do everything with your whole heart, Hailey. Don't stop now. We'll make a new contract."

"How long will this one last?" She gasped, finally open for him. Wet and welcome. Home.

"Forever."

"FOREVER?" HER VOICE broke on the word. Did he hear the fear in it? Did he hear the longing? "We couldn't even last three whole days, Lock."

"Keaton," he said quietly. "Call me Keaton."

A hysterical laugh. "Is that your real name? I don't even know. And your hand is…is…"

"Stroking your sweet cunt. I can feel you clenching deep in there. Makes my dick so fucking hard. It hurts, baby."

"Good," she moaned. Let him suffer—because God, it had hurt so much to leave him. She wanted him to feel it too.

She forced herself to focus. Even with his fingers slick and sliding. Even with her thighs vibrating, threatening to give out. She turned, her eyes searching his. "I don't know anything about you. You're the man behind the curtain. And you don't even have any special powers, do you? It's all a trick."

"I didn't need special powers to send you home, sweetheart. You did that yourself."

Her heart clenched. And look where that had gotten her. Alone. Afraid. It felt like a desert—as hot and barren as one— and he was just a mirage. So why did he feel so damn real? "Why are you here?"

"For this." With a sudden twist of his body, he shoved her

against the wall, between two smooth wooden pillars. He rocked against her, blocking her from sight, letting her feel his erection, wholly inappropriate in the vestibule of the church. Just like the fingers running through her wetness, messing her all up—a sweet communion.

"You ever come here?" he asked.

She didn't register his meaning at first—not until he pinched her clit. "No," she gasped.

"Not even once? No making out in the confessional?"

God, he wouldn't let up. Circling and circling until her hips were moving in tandem. "No, we're not…not Catholic. Don't confess."

"That's a shame, sweetheart. I'd love to hear those wicked thoughts of yours."

She shook her head—hard. "I've always been good. Always tried to be good."

Even though she'd failed. He was her serpent, luring her out of the garden, but she wasn't mad. She didn't want to stay locked up anymore. Eden was just a pretty prison when you got down to it.

His fingers sped up, moving with her hips. His voice was low in her ear. "If I sat next to you during service, I'd slip my hand under your skirt and touch you right there, in front of everyone."

She moaned, clutching his arm.

"Shh. You have to be quiet. You can't let them know what I'm doing to you."

His words spun the picture. She shuddered, imagining a packed chapel and staid sermon. And right beside her—Lock. Or Keaton. Her personal weakness and unlikely salvation.

His fingers plunged inside her, thumb relentless on her clit, and she shattered. She broke apart, crying his name—Keaton. She rocked against his hand and dug her nails into his back and used him just as much as he used her. He anchored her in the storm. He whipped her with wind and breathless pleasure. He was inside and out and all around her, slicking the air with salt and sex.

The climax stole her breath and gave it back in gasps and soft whimpers. He soothed her when her body jumped, petting her until the orgasm had passed, leaving her wrung out and slumped against the wall. His kiss against her forehead felt like a benediction, but his damp fingers pressing into her mouth made it even sweeter.

"Suck," he murmured, but she was already licking his fingers clean, turning the tables so that lust fired in his eyes. The bulge pressing against her hip proved he hadn't finished yet. And wouldn't finish—not until they'd figured this out.

That old contract was null and void. The new negotiations…well, she had a few tricks in her bag. Like tugging his head down so he could taste her on her tongue. Like nipping his lips so he groaned and humped her urgently.

She smiled. "Forever is a very long time."

"Hailey, you are not—"

"Boring. I know." She straightened her clothes, grateful for the dark nook he kept her in. He was always taking care of her, even when he didn't want her to know it. "But what if I'm the one who gets bored?"

A slow grin spread over his face. "Is that a challenge?"

She shrugged. "All those parties and groupies. There's a whole world to explore."

His hand cupped between her legs, over the fabric. "I'll take you anywhere you want to go. But no one sees this except for me."

"Never?" she said, thinking of his command at the concert. That had been fun.

"Unless I order you to," he amended.

Her wicked smile matched his. "Can I get that in writing?"

"I wouldn't have it any other way."

EPILOGUE

LOCK PUSHED THROUGH the crowd, ignoring his red-faced agent's shouts about photo ops and fan-club obligations, and raced for the rear exit. Let the other guys helm the PR machine for the night. Only one obligation mattered.

He was a mess after a full set and two encores, but they'd booked the chapel for midnight. No time for a shower or a change of clothes. He peeled his shirt off and used it to wipe his face, smearing eyeliner and sweat.

Two burly men with security vests propped open the door. The crowd outside sprang to life with shouts and camera flashes. A young woman burst through the throng, yanking her top down to expose a Sharpie pen tucked between generous cleavage. "Mark me, please."

The only woman he wanted to mark was waiting in the back of the limo parked a few feet away. The bodyguard by his side shouldered between them. "No autographs, ma'am."

He used her momentary meltdown to make a dash for the limo. For Hailey.

As soon as the door shut behind him, he relaxed and let the stage persona slip. *Lock has left the building.* Keaton Shaw melted into his woman's warm embrace, the brush of her lips, the sweet scent of her presence, totally oblivious to their audience.

"Not in front of the baby!" Chloe said, covering the sleeping infant's eyes and making an exaggerated O with her mouth. Tim, decked out in a powder-blue tuxedo, smirked and shook his head.

"Good show?" Hailey asked.

"Not the same without you in the wings."

"We had important business to attend to tonight. And sister stuff."

"Um, and sister stuff isn't important business?" Chloe teased. The baby let out a tiny squeak, and Keaton prayed it wouldn't start bawling.

"Of course it is. And mommy stuff." Hailey cooed, leaning over to peek at the little scream machine gurgling on Chloe's lap. At three months that kid could hold his own with a thrash metal band. And he was kind of cute when he started blowing those little bubbles at the corners of his mouth. Keaton decided he should get him an agent. Probably one less vicious than his own.

"And wardrobe. I better get big brownie points for this," Tim added, tugging at the hot-pink cummerbund wrapped around his waist.

"If by points you mean trifle, then yes." Chloe patted Tim's belly and turned back to them. "Are you guys ready? I'm ready. I can't thank you enough for doing this. Especially after we eloped on *you* last year."

Hailey squeezed Keaton's knee and grinned. "The timing worked out perfectly. The tour stop and Tim's break from Youth Nation."

Keaton snorted. Tim was a good guy, but ribbing him was too much fun to resist. "Church camp."

"Nondenominational youth outreach program," Tim corrected.

"Yes, you mold them and I warp them. I'm keeping you in business, buddy."

"You don't warp them; you give them an outlet for their pain."

"Don't get all deep on me now, Pastor Tim. There's time for that at the ceremony later."

"Don't call him that," Chloe and Hailey said in unison, giggling.

"Not yet, anyway. But, soon," Chloe added.

The limo stopped, and the driver lowered the privacy window. "Sir, we've arrived."

His heart raced the way it did before he stepped onstage. His palms tingled. Hailey threaded her fingers with his and squeezed. A warm calm spread through his chest. He'd made a lot of poor choices in his life, but this wasn't one of them. "I feel a little silly, shirtless and filthy, while you guys are glammed up."

Tim leaned forward. "I got you covered. There's tux rental inside."

"Absolutely not!" Hailey shrieked. "I want you exactly like this. Think of the pictures."

And he did. Her all in white—from the princess dress down to the fishnets—and him, half-naked and exposed. His heart ached with the sweetness of it.

"Oh, I almost forgot. For luck." Hailey tucked a scrap of blue satin into his pocket, her eyes flashing mischief. Were those panties? He checked. They were.

He hauled her into his lap, laughing, rucking up her dress, digging his fingers into the netting on her thighs. "Baby, I don't need luck—I don't need anything—as long as I have you."

THE END

THANK YOU!

Thank you for reading Three Nights with a Rockstar. We hope you enjoyed the ride. We appreciate anything you do to help spread the word about the Half-Life series, including leaving a review or recommending it to a friend.

The next book in the series, One Kiss with a Rock Star, will feature bass player Krist and his own personal pop princess. If you'd like to get notified when it comes out, sign up for Amber's newsletter at authoramberlin.com or Shari's newsletter at sharislade.com. Or both!

WANT A BACKSTAGE PASS?

Visit halflifebooks.com for band extras and behind-the-scenes
access to Lock, Krist and Moe from Half-Life!

PLAYLIST

1. Naïve by The Kooks
2. Demons by Imagine Dragons
3. Miserable by Lit
4. I Hope You Suffer by AFI
5. The Mother We Share by CHVRCHES
6. Strip Me by Natasha Beddingfield
7. Devil In Me by Kate Voegele
8. Sail by AWOLNATION
9. Vinegar & Salt by Hooverphonic
10. Pour Some Sugar On Me by Emm Gryner
11. Can't Help Falling in Love by Ingrid Michaelson
12. I Just Wanna Run by The Downtown Fiction
13. Blow It All Away by Sia
14. Fade Into You by Mazzy Star
15. Whirring by The Joy Formidable

ALSO BY AMBER LIN

Giving It Up

Allie prowls the club for a man who will use her hard and then ditch her. Hey, it's not rape if she wants it. Instead she finds Colin, who looks tough but treats her tenderly, despite her protests.

He tempts her, but kindness and a few mindblowing orgasms aren't enough to put her back together again. Two years ago her best friend betrayed her in the worst possible way; she'd be stupid to trust a man again. Especially one like Colin, whose criminal past threatens them both.

When her rapist returns, Allie must fight for the man she loves—and her life—hoping her newfound power will be enough to save them all.

EXCERPT FROM
GIVING IT UP

I set down the cup on the cracked countertop and stood to kiss him. I started off light, teasing, hoping to inflame him. This was all calculated, a game of risk and power.

He kissed me back softly, gently, like he didn't know we'd started playing. He held his body still, but his mouth roamed over mine, skimming and tasting.

It wasn't a magical kiss. Angels didn't sing, and nothing caught fire. But he wasn't too rough or too wet or too anything, and for me it was perfection.

I rubbed against him, undulating to a rhythm born of practice. His hands came up, one to cup my face, the other around my body.

I sighed.

He walked me backward, and we made out against the round fake-wood table, his hands running over my sides, my back. Avoiding the good parts like we were two horny teenagers in our parents' basements, new to this. I shuddered at the thought. This was all wrong. His hands were too light. I was half under him already, my hips cradling his, so I surged up and nipped at his lip. Predictably his body jerked, and he thrust his hips down onto me.

Yes. That's what I need. I softened my body, surrendering to him.

"Bed," he murmured against my lips.

We stripped at the same time, both eager. I wanted to see his body, to witness what he offered me, but it was dark in the room. Then he kissed me back onto the bed, and there was no more time to wonder. The cheap bedspread was rough and cool against my skin. His hands stroked over my breasts and then played gently with my nipples.

My body responded, turning liquid, but something was wrong.

I'd had this problem before. Not everyone wanted to play rough, but I was surprised that I'd misread him. His muscles were hard, the pads of his fingers were calloused. I didn't know how he could touch me so softly. Everything about him screamed that he could hurt me, so why didn't he?

I wanted him to have his nasty way with me, but every sweet caress destroyed the illusion. My fantasy was to let him do whatever he wanted with me, but not this.

"Harder," I said. "I need it harder."

Instead his hands gentled. The one that had been holding my breast traced the curve around and under.

I groaned in frustration. "What's wrong?"

He reached down, still breathing heavily, and pressed a finger lightly to my cunt, then stroked upward through the moisture. I gasped, rocking my hips to follow his finger.

"You like this," he said.

Yes, I liked it. I was undeniably aroused but too aware. I needed the emptiness of being taken. "I like it better rough."

Colin frowned. My eyes widened at the ferocity of his expression.

In one smooth motion he flipped me onto my stomach. I lost my breath from the surprise and impact. His left hand slid under my body between my legs and cupped me. His right hand fisted in my hair, pulling my head back. His erection throbbed beside my ass in promise. I wanted to beg him to fuck me, but all I could do was gasp. He didn't need to be told, though, and ground against me, using my hair as a handle.

That small pain on my scalp was perfection, sharp and sweet. Numbness spread through me, as did relief.

The pain dimmed. My arousal did too, but that was okay. I was only vaguely aware of him continuing to work my body from behind.

I went somewhere else in my mind. I'd stay that way all night.

At least that's what usually happened.

Want to read more? Giving It Up is available now from Amazon.com, BarnesAndNoble.com and other book retailers.

ALSO BY SHARI SLADE

The Opposite of Nothing

Callie Evans would rather hide out in her DJ sound booth than face the fact that she's in love with her best friend, notorious campus hottie Tayber King.

Tayber turns hooking up into an art form—no drama, no commitment, no lies, and nobody gets hurt. Nobody but Callie, that is. When she sees an opportunity to explore his sexier side using a fake online profile, she grabs it. Now her uninhibited alter-ego 'Sasha' is steaming up the screen, and Callie is breaking all of Tayber's rules.

As Callie and Tayber get closer, online and off, she knows she has to confess. And risk losing him forever.

EXCERPT FROM
THE OPPOSITE OF NOTHING

She changed into a tank top and threadbare shorts before slipping into her desk chair. *I'll just check my school email, ten minutes tops.* She was lying to herself, bargaining with the devil. *I will not open his profile. I will not send him a message.* Making that fake profile for herself last month had seemed like such a good idea at two o'clock in the morning, after a few beers with Jessa and a few agonizing hours of watching Tayber hook up with some random girl at The Brick. She just wanted to know what she was missing. In graphic detail. *Sasha* let her find out. Except it had only made her wanting worse, and it was such a wrong thing to do. So she'd stopped. At least a dozen times.

But nothing stopped him from messaging her. There it was, blinking away. She should ignore it. Delete, delete, delete. It wasn't even for her. Not really. It was for Sasha. And she'd sworn she'd never be Sasha again.

Tay: Hey

How could three tiny letters be so suggestive? She could hear him in her head. He'd say it kind of soft, but forceful, like the whole universe of his carnal experience could be contained in one word. She pictured him hunched over his laptop, shaggy hair eclipsing his face, shirtless, bare feet hanging off the end of his extra-long bed.

She had to answer. She wanted him any way she could have him.

Sasha: Hey yourself.

Tay: Why am I always happy to see you?

Sasha: Because I'm awesome like that?

Tay: You are. I'm looking at your picture right now. So beautiful.

Not me. She'd sent him a picture of her cousin, on spring break in Cabo three years ago, filling out her bikini and pulling a duck face for the camera.

Sasha: Not really

Tay: Inside and out

Sasha: Laying it on thick tonight?

Tay: I can't stop thinking about you.

It was torture. The ninth level of Hell. Everything she'd ever wanted him to say was there on the screen, except it wasn't really for her.

Tay: I wish I could touch you.

And she was burning, flaming. If he were saying these things in person, she'd disintegrate. She tugged on her tank top, pulling the thin cotton away from her itchy skin.

Tay: Is that okay?

She was practically molting, slipping right out of her skin on the spot. This disastrous attraction might kill her. She squeezed her thighs together and shifted in her seat.

Sasha: I want to touch you too.

Tay: Skype?

Sasha: Can't, still no webcam.

Shit. This was going to be the end of it, again. Who didn't have a webcam? She held her breath, waiting for the little indicator to flash that he was answering. A full minute. He was probably frustrated, pulling that mop of hair out of his face now, tugging it into a tiny ponytail. A minute and a half. He'd lost interest. Any second now his light would go out.

Tay: Too bad

She exhaled, a rush of relief that left her giddy.

Sasha: Sorry

Tay: Don't you want to see me?

Sasha: More than anything

Tay: I want to see my hands on you.

Was he touching himself now? She traced a figure eight over the soft skin below her navel, chasing the flutter building there. She'd never be able to tell him the truth, and this was never going to be enough.

Sasha: You're touching me now

Tay: Where?

Sasha: My belly

Tay: Lower. I'm touching you lower. I've got my fingers between your legs and you're so wet for me.

Want to read more? The Opposite of Nothing is available now from Amazon.com, BarnesAndNoble.com and other book retailers.

OTHER BOOKS
BY AMBER LIN

How to Say Goodbye
Betraying Mercy

The Half-Life Series
Three Nights with a Rock Star
One Kiss with a Rock Star

The Lost Girls Series
Giving It Up
Selling Out
Tempting Fate

Dearling, Texas Series
Chance of Rain

Men of Fortune Series
Letters at Christmas
Falling for the Pirate

OTHER BOOKS
BY SHARI SLADE

Copeland College Series
The Opposite of Nothing
Copeland College Novella #2

The Half-Life Series
Three Nights with a Rock Star
One Kiss with a Rock Star

Anthologies
Summer Rain

ABOUT THE AUTHORS

Amber Lin writes edgy romance with damaged hearts, redemptive love, and a steamy ever after. Her debut novel, Giving It Up, received The Romance Review's Top Pick, Night Owl Top Pick, and 5 Blue Ribbons from Romance Junkies. RT Book Reviews gave it 4.5 stars, calling it "truly extraordinary." Since then, she has gone on to write erotic, contemporary, and historical romances.

To stay up to date with upcoming releases, sign up for her newsletter at authoramberlin.com.

Shari Slade is a snarky optimist. A would-be academic with big dreams and very little means. When she isn't toiling away in the non-profit sector, she's writing gritty stories about identity and people who make terrible choices in the name of love (or lust). Somehow, it all works out in the end. If she had a patronus it would be a platypus.

Sign up for her newsletter at sharislade.com to stay up-to-date on all the latest releases, happenings, and events.

ACKNOWLEDGEMENTS

A huge thank you to Del Dryden, Lea Shafer, and Sharon Muha for the boot polish and elbow grease. We appreciate your help making this book shine.

COPYRIGHT

Made in the USA
Charleston, SC
18 June 2014